Glory Be!

JANET LAMBERT

Decorations by
WOODI ISHMAEL

Image Cascade Publishing
www.ImageCascade.com

MANUFACTURED IN THE UNITED STATES
OF AMERICA

A hardcover edition of this book was originally published by E. P. Dutton & Co. It is here reprinted by arrangement with Mrs. Jeanne Ann Vanderhoef.

First *Image Cascade Publishing* edition published 2001.
Copyright renewed © 1971 by Jeanne Ann Vanderhoef.

Library of Congress Cataloging in Publication Data
Lambert, Janet, 1895–1973.
        Glory be!

(Juvenile Girls)
Reprint. Originally published: New York: E. P. Dutton, 1943.

ISBN 1-930009-28-3 (Pbk.)

FOR

MARY JANE

Books By Janet Lambert

PENNY PARRISH STORIES
Star Spangled Summer 1941
Dreams of Glory 1942
Glory Be! 1943
Up Goes the Curtain 1946
Practically Perfect 1947
The Reluctant Heart 1950

TIPPY PARRISH STORIES
Miss Tippy 1948
Little Miss Atlas 1949
Miss America 1951
Don't Cry Little Girl 1952
Rainbow After Rain 1953
Welcome Home, Mrs. Jordon 1953
Song in Their Hearts 1956
Here's Marny 1969

JORDON STORIES
Just Jennifer 1945
Friday's Child 1947
Confusion by Cupid 1950
A Dream for Susan 1954
Love Taps Gently 1955
Myself & I 1957
The Stars Hang High 1960
Wedding Bells 1961
A Bright Tomorrow 1965

PARRI MACDONALD STORIES
Introducing Parri 1962
That's My Girl 1964
Stagestruck Parri 1966
My Davy 1968

CANDY KANE STORIES
Candy Kane 1943
Whoa, Matilda 1944
One for the Money 1946

DRIA MEREDITH STORIES
Star Dream 1951
Summer for Seven 1952
High Hurdles 1955

CAMPBELL STORIES
The Precious Days 1957
For Each Other 1959
Forever and Ever 1961
Five's a Crowd 1963
First of All 1966
The Odd Ones 1969

SUGAR BRADLEY STORIES
Sweet as Sugar 1967
Hi, Neighbor 1968

CHRISTIE DRAYTON STORIES
Where the Heart Is 1948
Treasure Trouble 1949

PATTY AND GINGER STORIES
We're Going Steady 1958
Boy Wanted 1959
Spring Fever 1960
Summer Madness 1962
Extra Special 1963
On Her Own 1964

CINDA HOLLISTER STORIES
Cinda 1954
Fly Away Cinda 1956
Big Deal 1958
Triple Trouble 1965
Love to Spare 1967

Dear Readers:

Mother always said she wanted her books to be good enough to be found in someone's attic!

After all of these years, I find her stories—not in attics at all—but prominent in fans' bookcases just as mine are. It is so heart-warming to know that through these republications she will go on telling good stories and being there for her "girls," some of whom find no other place to turn.

With a heart full of love and pride–
Janet Lambert's daughter,
Jeanne Ann Vanderhoef

CONTENTS

Glory Be!

★

CHAPTER I

Good-by, Dear Youth

Trudy squeezed a pink rosebud onto the white icing of a cake and remarked glumly: "Seems like it ain't no use wastin' time fixin' the cake up so fancy when Miss Penny is dead set against havin' a birthday." Her brown face lifted and she stared unseeingly through a window at the bare trees. "Miss Penny jes' nachelly don't want to grow up," she sighed.

"I know." Mrs. Parrish, busy at the table behind her, searched out candles and holders from a large box. She looked at Trudy's straight old back and asked with a smile, "What shall I do? There are plenty of yellow holders, or blue, but I can't find eighteen pink ones. Penny will have a fit if they aren't pink."

"They ought to be there." Trudy laid down her pastry tube and came to look at the bright piles. "I had twenty-one for Mr. David's birthday. I know, 'cause I thought red, white and blue would look better for a young gen'man about to graduate from West Point; but he said Miss Carrol liked pink—so we had pink."

13

"Love is wonderful, isn't it, Trudy?" Marjorie Parrish spoke lightly but her brown eyes were full of happiness for David. "I can't believe that David could actually fall in love with our best friend's daughter, and with a girl who is already like another daughter to me." She, too, looked out at the dull winter scene and added, "I hope, though, they won't want to marry as soon as David graduates. A second lieutenant's pay isn't very large and they're both so young. Then too, Carrol's father would be so alone without her."

"Yas'm, Mr. Houghton sets a heap o' store by that child." Trudy counted the pink holders again and shook her head. "I reckon you's got to go to the Post Exchange," she said.

"Oh Trudy!" Marjorie Parrish pushed back her hair that matched her eyes, looking dolefully at the colored woman who had managed her family for twenty years. "Don't make me go out again in this vile weather," she pleaded. "Colonel Parrish has the big car. Ever since he got promoted to a lieutenant colonel, the car seems to have become a part of his rank. And Penny and Carrol are off, heaven knows where, in the little one. Send Bobby."

"He's gone to scout meetin'."

"And Tippy?" Mrs. Parrish knew it was hopeless but she had to ask.

"She tooken her paper dolls and went to the Mc-Guires. Miz Parrish, you're goin' to have a more unhappy child than you got if you don't have pink candles."

"I suppose so." She dumped the odd candles back into the box and said, with a comical look at Trudy, "But it does seem to me that an old woman with a husband and four children, a house guest that's almost another child, two cars and a police dog, could find someone to do her errands."

"An old woman? Pshaw!" Trudy dropped the pastry tube again, and with her hands folded over her big white apron, prepared herself for a lecture. "Here you is . . ."

"I know it, Trudy, darling, don't say it." Her victim flashed a smile that brought dimples into her cheeks. "I'm so young I'll run all the way to the Post Exchange."

"Well, that's more like it. What would Major . . . 'Scuse me, Colonel Parrish say if he was to come in an' find you old an' settin' down when he's so spry?"

"He'd feel sorry for me." She was in the hall coat closet now and her voice was muffled as she bent over an assortment of goloshes, hunting for a matched pair. "He'd say . . ."

"What would he say? Something too, too tender, I'll bet."

Marjorie Parrish straightened, glanced at the door and there stood Penny. Penny's cheeks were pink from a brisk November wind, her hair had blown in a brown swirl from under her woolly parka, and her brown eyes were laughing as she looked on the havoc her mother had wrought in the closet. "If you're looking for your goloshes," she added, "I have them on."

"Well, that's fine." Her mother threw down an overshoe and snapped off the light. "You can do an errand for me," she said. "Where's Carrol?"

"She's out in the car."

"Well, for goodness' sake, what is she sitting out there for?"

"She's waiting to go on the errand." Penny pushed back her hair and grinned at her mother fondly. "We always do errands all day long when we have a birthday. What's this one?"

"We haven't enough candle holders for the cake, and I want you to tell your father, if you can find him any place around the post, not to forget the—the surprise."

"Umhum, I know, the ice cream." Penny chuckled at her mother's lack of subtlety. "I just saw Dad and reminded him. He's down at the riding hall watching your son and some thirty odd cadets going around at a slow trot, ho-o-o'." She poked her head into the kitchen, her smile fading as she studied the pile of pink candles on the porcelain table.

"I'll tell you what, Trudy," she said with a sigh. "Put a circle of blue candles in the middle like a little

16

forget-me-not. Five of them—for all the good years I've had in my teens. I'd like that better anyway."

She took off her parka, then went slowly along the hall, down the steps and across the lawn, to the car that was parked in the driveway.

"We don't have to go any place," she said to the girl who was leaning out the car window. Then her head went down on the sill and she began to cry.

"Why Penny." Carrol Houghton bent over, her pale curls brushing against Penny's brown mane. Her blue eyes that held the magic of a violet bed seen through a dark encircling hedge, were filled with tender sympathy. Her beauty, breath-taking in its clear-cut perfection, was warmed by a loving smile. "Silly little Penny Parrish," she said gently, "afraid of growing up."

Penny lifted her head, fumbled for a handkerchief then wiped her eyes on her red mitten. "You don't understand," she said. "No one does, not even you. It's all been so swell. Every year of my life—and now it's going to be different."

"What's going to be so different about it?" A small dimple that acted as a traffic light at one corner of Carrol's mouth flashed out and halted a smile. "To-day's no different than yesterday or last week."

"But it is." Penny's head bobbed up and down with vigor. "You see now I'll have to stop my junior college work at Briarcliff."

"But why?" Carrol's eyes were wide with surprise. "You just started three months ago."

"I know." Penny opened the door and as Carrol moved over, climbed in beside her. They sat in the car, two furry figures in their skunk coats, and Penny looked up and down the street at the square brick houses on their wide lawns; all alike, and each bearing a neat sign fastened below the steps with the number of the quarters, the officer's name who occupied it, and his rank.

"I've always loved living in the army," she began. "And I've always known that sometime I'd have to leave it. David was eighteen when he came to West Point and I was almost fifteen when we moved here. I guess I decided that fall that when I was eighteen I'd start my career, too, just like he did."

"But Penny, he'll be twenty-two when he begins his career." Carrol thought of the dear tall blondness of David and wished he were here to tease Penny out of one of her dramatic moods. She looked hopefully up the street but no gray-coated figure was on its empty walks. So she sighed and listened to Penny saying:

"I know, but he began preparing at eighteen. I don't know how to be an actress yet. I have to learn. And I can't learn until I start, and when I start it's the beginning of the end of the army." Penny put her hands in her pockets, slid down into the seat and sat

18

looking at the fur on her goloshes. "I guess the truth of the matter," she said dolefully into the silence, "is that I'm just scared to start."

Carrol's laughter rippled out over the cold dusk. "This is one day you've marked on your calendar with an X," she teased in what she hoped was the attack David would take. "You're going to suffer it all out in one day, and then tomorrow you'll go about the business of doing what you have wanted to do since you were able to walk. Penny, can't you see that, darling? You're dramatizing this and enjoying it no end."

"Am I?" Penny looked up in surprise. "You mean I'm acting? I can't be, because it hurts."

"Of course it does. I hate to tell you this, but I suppose that's why you *will* be famous some day, just as you've always declared you would. You never know whether you're suffering or pretending."

"But I should." Penny's flying locks nodded again. "That's what I have to learn. I'll never get any place if I stand up on the stage and suffer with every character. But I still wish I hadn't set eighteen as the time to begin."

"You have twelve more months of eighteen, pet," Carrol reminded her. "So take it easy."

She saw a tall cadet far down the block and her heart skipped a beat as she thought of the career she, herself, had chosen. Penny, as if reading her thoughts, asked wonderingly: "Will you be satisfied living in the army, Carrol, on a second lieutenant's pay, after having had Gladstone and a staff of servants, and a penthouse in New York?"

"I'll hate leaving Daddy," Carrol answered, watching the approaching figure that swung along as no one but David could, "but the money doesn't matter. I'll have David."

Penny searched Carrol's face in wonder. David was a very nice brother. He was, in fact, such a wonderful brother that no other boy had ever been quite perfect in Penny's eyes; but she doubted that life with him in a small apartment would be worth the sacrifice of a summer home like Gladstone, a winter estate in Florida, and a three-floor apartment in New York. Her eyes followed Carrol's and she leaned out to shout:

"Hi, David!"

"Hello." David came to the car and kissed her. "Many happy returns," he said. "Gosh, you're young." He looked across her at Carrol and his eyes held a secret greeting. "Prettier than ever," he declared solemnly. "Every day I think it can't be possible, but by gum, it is."

"What a stunning speech." Penny answered before Carrol could speak. "I wish someone could say that to me."

"Well, you aren't hard to look at." David surveyed her critically. Penny was vivid, he reflected. Every mood flashed across her face. Her eyes caught a thought, held it until the last bubble of joy died away, or until tears quenched its misery. Her mouth was sweet and generous, and her chin cupped in the palm of his hand, was small with a soft determined roundness. He tweeked the end of her short straight nose and added laconically: "You're okay."

"Thanks." Penny pushed against the brass buttons of his gray cadet overcoat and swung open the door. "You two can sit here in the cold if you like," she said, "but I'm going in to have a happy birthday."

David went around to open the door for Carrol, smiling at her as she got out. "Was the conference Penny trouble?" he asked in an understanding murmur.

"Umhum. I tried to talk to her the way you do but I don't know whether I did very well, or not. She thinks she should start her career."

"I thought that would happen pretty soon." David leaned his hand against the car and searched the lovely face upturned to his. "Have you had any regrets about not going to Vassar this fall?"

"Not a one. My staying with Daddy this year means so much to him, and to me too, that college doesn't even tempt me. Perhaps next year . . ."

"Would you mind skipping it then if someone else, say if I, asked you to?" David's head was bent to hers and she answered softly:

"I'd skip it forever, David."

"Then let's consider it skipped." He took her hand in his and waved them both at the headlights turning into the drive. "Hello, Dad," he called. "That was a good class this afternoon."

Colonel Parrish stepped from the car, reached inside for a freezer of ice cream, grinning over his shoulder as they came to him. "Hello, children." He passed the freezer to David, and walking to the house beside them, put his arm around Carrol. "Has that busy father of yours shown up yet?" he asked.

"Not yet, but he'll be along." She smiled at him and suggested that David use the back door for Penny's "surprise" which would be a surprise to her only in flavor. Then she stopped on the steps beside the man who looked enough like David to be his handsome older brother. "Uncle Dave," she said, using a title that had changed the Parrishes and Houghtons from mere friends into a close little family of loving relatives, "when Daddy comes will you ask him if he's seen a doctor?"

"Do you think there's something wrong, Carrol?" Quick concern leaped into Colonel Parrish's eyes, but she answered quietly:

"I don't know. He looks frightfully thin and we don't go out as much as we used to. Perhaps he's only tired."

"I'll have a talk with him." He gave her a pat and

added: "I wouldn't worry about it. He's so tall that even a pound off will show."

"I know it. Thank you, Uncle Dave."

She went into the long, lovely living room to admire the tooth curly-headed Tippy was proudly displaying in a moist, pink palm, and to examine the hole it had left in Tippy's rosebud mouth. She inspected Bobby's new Scout badge and stood with Penny before her table of gifts. But when the door opened and her father's deep voice joined Colonel Parrish's in the hall she dropped the yellow sweater she was holding.

"Daddy!" she cried, running to him. Her arms reached out, and the dark man, distinguished, with graying hair at the temples, caught her to him.

"I never get over the wonder of it, Marjorie," he grinned over her head to Mrs. Parrish, who was coming down the stairs. "I've had her for three years—and isn't it tragic that I didn't know you sooner so you could show me what a fool I was for the other sixteen?"

"It made you both finer people. Carrol got splendid care at her grandmother's and it taught you, Langdon, how much you need her." Mrs. Parrish took his hand, turning to nod to the colored orderly who was hovering in the dining room door. "Are you ready for us, Yates?"

"Yes, ma'am. Evenin', Colonel Parrish. Evenin', Mr. Houghton. Won't you rest your coat, sir?"

GLORY BE!

Yates whisked away the overcoat, his mind in a whirl from his complicated speech, but proud of the air with which he had delivered it. He served dinner with a neat professional touch that matched his white coat, if not his heavy army shoes and soldier slacks. He liked to listen to the conversation. He liked to help Tippy with the cutting of her meat; to feel a part of this family around the candle-lighted table. "They's havin' a good time," he told Trudy on one of his trips to the kitchen, "but that door bell ought to start ringin'. I can't keep passin' things forever."

As though he had commanded it, a ringing peal answered him and he clumped heartily down the hall. A twitch of his coat gave him the same proud look of the Houghtons' English butler, and he threw the door wide. Six long strides got him to the dining room ahead of entering guests, and his voice raised above a din, announced happily: "Some ladies and gentlemen is callin'."

"Happy birthday! Happy birthday!"

Yates was swept aside but he was busy with fur coats, cadet coats, scarves and caps, and his grin was wide.

"Darlings!" Penny bounced from her chair, adding herself to the crowd in the door. "Denise, you lamb! And Faith, bless your heart! Imagine you coming all the way up here from New York! Hi, Dick, Mike—and Bob, of all things. What pass got you out, you lowly second classman?" Her hands were reaching to every-one, her eyes dancing.

"It's Saturday night, nut," Michael told her on his way to speak to those still at the table. "I was under the impression we had a date tonight."

"So we have." Penny hugged Denise who was near-est her. Once, three years ago, she had thought Denise Dane a mousy little thing; now, she was a very dear friend. "What do you hear from a certain young lieutenant who used to beau you about?" she asked as everyone followed Michael into the dining room.

"Steve? He may get leave next month and if he does, he's coming East." Denise's small plain face lighted up and Penny hugged her again.

"Swell." Then she pursued Faith Carmichael around the table where she was standing, blondly pale and lovely, beside Mrs. Parrish. "You and Dee will spend the night, won't you?" she crowded in to ask.

"Do you want us?" Faith turned her cameo-perfect face inquiringly.

"Of course we do."

"Then I may as well tell you—we've already planned to stay."

"Well, I like that!" Penny grinned and nodded to Yates who would relay the arrival of overnight guests to Trudy, then turned her attention to the boys.

She saw they wore their full dress, ready for the

evening; their coat tails dotted with brass buttons; their chests gleaming with them, too, in orderly rows that reached to their high collars. Their hair, Michael's so black, Dick's so flaming red, and Bob's so sandy, was brushed smoothly back from their foreheads. Michael wore the dark red sash of a cadet lieutenant, knotted and hanging against the stiff gray of his trousers; Bob's sleeve bore a sergeant's stripes, the highest rank of his class; but Dick was apparently happy as a private. Later, when David dressed, he too would wear a sash, and would have the added rank of captain of his company.

"How about some ice cream?" she asked.

"Yates is serving the birthday cake in the living room," her mother answered her. She rose from the table and as the others chattered through the door, put her arm around Penny. "This is the surprise I really meant," she said. "Are you happier, now?"

"I'm *practically* overcome." Penny used the childish word that had seen her through so many times of difficult self-expression, then pressed a light kiss on her mother's cheek. "Being eighteen isn't so bad," she said, giving Bobby a forward push, "it's only getting used to the idea. Thanks, Mums, for starting me out with a lift."

★

CHAPTER II

BRIGHT LIGHTS OF DREAMS

Penny spent several days considering the problem of her career. It had been easy to boast that, now she was eighteen, she would embark upon the life of which she had dreamed—but how to begin that life was another matter. She had no doubt that hundreds of young actresses, as hopeful and as talented as she was, were trudging the sidewalks of Broadway; and while she was eager to join the throng, she knew that a promenade would only end in a cup of tea at Schrafft's. There were doors she must enter, managers she must brave. No one could become famous simply by walking among the professionals.

"I don't know what to do about it," she sighed to herself one Friday afternoon. "Perhaps I'd better go to New York and talk it over with Carrol."

"Why don't you go down with David," her mother suggested when Penny broached the subject to her. "He has a long week-end and is planning to take a bus."

GLORY BE!

"He is? Well for goodness' sake, imagine his trying to get away without me!"

She was down the stairs, in her car, and rolling up and down the winding roads of West Point, forming her attack as she went. It would be an attack she knew, for David's week-ends were few and far between and he might not relish sharing one with a member of his family. She swung around a curve, past the chapel that shone whitely on its hill, dipped for a view of the riding hall above the swift-flowing Hudson river, and slammed on her brakes before Grant Hall, which was the meeting place of girls and cadets.

"Please call out Cadet Parrish, D.G., Company A," she panted to the cadet who, as Junior Officer of the Guard, sat behind a desk at the door. Then she whisked into the Boodler's, the soda fountain that catered to the corps, and dropped down at a table. She was enjoying a malted milk and three of David's classmates when he ambled to the door.

"Oh, David, come here quickly!" she cried when she saw him lose interest in the identity of his unknown caller. "I'm going to New York with you."

If he had been happy to see her, and it was rather doubtful that he was, Penny having a disturbing way of breaking into his day—her words were a magician's wand that changed his smile to a frown. "Now listen, Pen," he began, tossing his cap onto a vacant chair and leaning across the table, "I'm going off on a holiday."

"So am I, Davy, that's what I'm trying to tell you. Mums suggested it." Penny's grin was wide, her hands covered his on the table and she bent toward him. "Aren't you happy about it?"

"Not much." David looked hopefully at the circle of corps mates. "Wouldn't one of you like to entertain her tonight?" he offered. "I can't get any kick out of having a date with my girl and dragging along the kid sister."

"Why, David Parrish, I think you're mean." Penny sat back, her laughter belying her words. "What time do we go?" she asked.

"The bus I'm taking leaves at six." David reached for her glass, rested his foot on the rung of a chair, and looked at the others. "Haven't any of you got a pass for New York?" he asked again, over the glass's rim. "Even Penny's better than a blind date."

But none of them had a pass for New York, or any other place, so they sat glumly by while David reluctantly accepted her entrance into his plans.

"Okay. You can pick me up in time for the bus," he conceded, tossing her a Boodler's check from the book he carried in his cap. "But remember, you're on your own tonight. No horning in on Carrol and me." He replaced an odd assortment of impedimenta in a handkerchief, wedged the whole back into his cap, grinned at her and departed.

"Sweet, isn't he?" Penny remarked happily as she slipped into her coat. "I hope you're all kinder to your sisters."

She dashed out to her car again, serenely sure that she was laying the cornerstone of a magnificent structure that would be her future. By merely setting foot in the magic city of her dreams she would begin her building. Two hours on a bus with David, listening to his sound advice, his understanding interest, would give her courage. And perhaps, she thought, any moment the big chance might come.

"Exciting things are going to happen," she told the gathering dusk. "I just feel it—as Trudy says, 'I jes' feel it in my bones.'"

She chattered all the way to New York, forgetting that it was David's advice she sought, while he listened with an amused tolerance. And it was only when he was helping her on with her coat that he gave her a pat and a bit of, unasked, advice.

"Take it easy, Pen," he cautioned. "You can get everything you want out of life—but be darn sure you know *what* it is you want."

"But I do know." Penny looked at the tall buildings from the taxi window, wondering how David could doubt her future. It was all there; winging its way over the air from broadcasting stations, flashing across footlights, twinkling in hundreds of signs before motion picture houses. And as she stepped from the elevator into the Houghton penthouse she knew that it was here too; in Perkins, the butler, in soft rugs, in the book-lined library, in beauty and gracious living. Once, in a childish way, she had envied Carrol this richness; now, or some day, she corrected herself with an honest grin, she would have its duplicate. And it would all be hers through the attainment of her heart's desire.

"Hi, pet," she grinned as Carrol gave her a hug. "I'm tagging."

"I'm glad you are." Carrol slipped her hand in David's, adding with a twinkle in her eye, "Because I have a surprise for you."

"A nice one?"

"It all depends." Carrol winked at David, laughed and baited Penny again. "It's one you gave me once. It wasn't so nice then—but I think we'll all enjoy it now. I put it in the sunroom."

"Well for Pete's sake, what is it?" She snatched off her hat and coat for Perkins, waited impatiently while David was divested of his cadet overcoat that seemed to have an endless number of buttons, and rushed through the drawing room ahead of them.

"Well, as I live and breathe," she cried, stopping in the sunroom door, "if it isn't the great Lieutenant Hayes, in person!"

"Hello, Penny." A tall young officer crossed the room to her, held out a hesitant hand, and asked with a rueful grin: "Are you still mad at me?"

Penny looked into blue eyes that were laughing at her. In a flash of embarrassment she remembered a Thanksgiving Day three years ago when she had brought Terry Hayes home to dinner, and by doing it had complicated the serenity of Carrol's and David's young love. "You were perfectly horrid," she said with her chin defiantly in the air, "and I was furious with you. But I forgive you now."

Her hand lay lightly in his but he gave it a squeeze before he released it for David. "Hello, fellow," he grinned, "how goes it?"

There was nothing apologetic about Terry Hayes. If once he had lavished more attention on Carrol than the aching heart of a lowly fourth classman could bear he showed no regret. And David, meeting him, told by a friendly hand on his shoulder that he had forgotten the matter.

"It's darn good to see you," he said frankly. "What are you doing around here?"

"I'm stationed at Fort Dix. Brought some enlisted men up to Governors Island, hence the uniform, and thought I'd give Carrol a ring to get the latest dope on you all. You look fit."

"I am. I'm just waiting until June when I can get into my job."

"Well, I hope you don't feel as green as I did." Terry sat down on a sofa, smiling across the room at Penny. "I was a mess, wasn't I, Pen? I needed you to tell me off."

Penny looked at him thoughtfully. Terry was just as handsome as ever and, she knew, just as conceited. Already he had focused the conversation on himself. He stole scenes. He wanted the center of the stage, and he wanted it alone. So she said evenly: "Perhaps. Although it wasn't my place to tell you." Then she turned to Carrol and asked: "What have you and David planned for tonight?"

"We thought we'd have dinner some place, go wherever our favorite band is playing, and dance. Terry suggested that you and he join us."

"Me?" Penny threw back her head and laughed. "Why, Terry," she teased, "with all the glamour girls in New York would you take me out? Remember my temper."

"With or without it, I'll take you. You know what I said to you just before I made my grand exit, don't you?" His eyes were level on hers, his head was tilted just enough to give a warm intimate appeal to his words, and to her horror Penny found herself blushing.

"Pooh," she retorted to hide her confusion, "now you're making fun of me."

She repeated that to Carrol a few moments later

when she was seated before the mirror in the bedroom they shared. "I don't mind going out with him," she said, dabbing powder on her nose, "although I really had intended to go to the theatre and think about my career. But he always gets me so fussed and makes me so darned uncomfortable."

Carrol, taking her coat from a hanger in the closet, turned to ask curiously: "What did he mean by his 'grand exit'? You've never told me."

"Nothing." Penny snapped her lipstick open and shut, staring at it. "It was after I had told him what I thought of him for making David jealous, and he said, 'and now you don't like me so much,' or something like that. And I said, 'no I don't,' and he said, 'well, that's queer, because now I like you more.' Ridiculous, wasn't it?" She put the lipstick back into her bag, forgetting to use it. "Maybe he liked me because I stood up to him," she mused.

"He probably did. At least, you were the first one he asked about when he called." Carrol slipped into her lynx jacket and came to stand beside the dressing table. "Hurry up," she urged. "He's fun and we'll have a good time."

"But he's old. He's four years older than David." Penny looked up in amazement. "My goodness," she said, making a wry face, "I never went out with a man before."

That Terry was older, was soon forgotten. His uniform was olive drab instead of the accustomed gray of the Point, but he looked as young as David. He laughed as much, was grave or gay with a charming lack of self-consciousness. Penny's antagonism gradually melted away, although she told herself, "If he so much as flirts one flirt with Carrol, I'm going to yank him home by the hair of his head." But watch as carefully as she could, Terry's smiles were only for her.

"Penny," he said, when they were dancing in a supper club, high above the lights of New York, "do you think you could like me again, and could respect me —the way you said you did when you were a kid?"

"Why . . ." She drew away from him to look at him seriously. "I do like you, Terry. I'm even enjoying you."

"But you don't feel about me as you did before that fateful Thanksgiving Day. You haven't thought so much of me, since."

"I haven't thought of you at all." She smiled up at him; then seeing his look of hurt pride, added with a chuckle: "Really, Terry, I've had kind of a busy life too, you know."

"Too busy to include me now?"

His blue eyes were too close to her, his arm about her too disturbing. "You're sweet, Pen," he went on.

"I told you once that some day you'd be a knock-out —that I'd be proud to say 'I knew her when.' Well, this is the 'when.'"

"Oh, Terry, you're such a flatterer." Penny sought vainly for a better retort, but he drew her to him, and as they spun among the dancers her chaotic thoughts whirled across his shoulder strap.

She wished for Michael; for the saneness of dancing with Michael, or Dick, or Bob. Terry understood girls too well. He's got too much of a line for me, she thought. The man's devastating. And I simply can't let him clutter up my life. So, when the music stopped with Terry still holding her hand, she turned to him and said as matter-of-factly as she could:

"Listen, Terry, I like you. I know all about the charm you can turn on—because, you must remember, I've seen you in action. You don't have to impress me, because I'm just Penny Parrish—the girl you've known a long, long time."

"And who still doesn't believe me."

He had the look of a small boy being unjustly punished for accidentally burning down the house, and Penny frowned at him in despair.

"Listen, darling," she said patiently, "I think you're swell. In fact, if it makes you happy to know it, you can start my heart going pit-a-pat." She saw his face light up and shot him a gamin grin. "But cadets can do it too, and I'm not having any."

"But you are." He still held her hand and he matched her smile with one of conquest mingled with amusement. "You're going to see a lot of me, because I'm going to hound you. I'm going to camp on your doorstep."

"Well, let's both camp at the table first."

She turned, and as he walked beside her toward Carrol and David, she wished she had stayed safely in West Point that night. "Emotional upsets aren't for me," she told herself as she listened to the easy banter of the other three. "I've got a goal ahead."

"Why so quiet?" David asked, when he noticed that her usual sparkle was dimmed. "Are you moping because I haven't asked you to dance?"

"If I am," Penny leaned back against the red upholstery and considered him, "I'd have such a chronic persecution complex that I could rent myself out as a hired mourner for funerals."

"Want to have a go around the outside?"

"I'll try to bear it, brother dear, for the honor of the family."

She stood up, but when David put his arm around her he wasted no time in proffering a brotherly lecture. "You're behaving like an idiot," he told her with brutal frankness. "Didn't you ever have anyone flirt with you before?"

"Huh?" Penny's head came up with a jerk.

"You act like a little girl who's never been out of the

nursery. Terry's throwing you the ball. Catch it, and wham it back at him—don't let it hit you between the eyes."

"Well, I am—I mean, I'm not. Oh Davy . . ." Penny's brown eyes were troubled. "I'm all mixed up in my mind. It isn't Terry any more than it's lots of other boys; Michael, for instance."

"You like Mike pretty much?"

"I've always liked Michael. But I'm planning a career. No one ever seems to remember that. They don't treat me with any *respect*."

David hugged her and laughed. He laughed so heartily that couples dancing near him smiled with him, thinking what a stunning pair the tall cadet and the slender, vivid girl made. A few even yearned for youth and the gay romance these two seemed to have. None of them heard David say: "Listen, dope. You're the kind who draws problems like water draws lightning. You stumble along with your eyes on a goal that's miles ahead of you. You'll probably have a career, I don't know; but there's no use missing all the scenery as you go along."

"You mean, I'm too serious about it?"

"Sure. Take it easy." They danced a few bars in silence before he added: "I don't mean, fall for Hayes —heavens, I hope you have too much sense for that! But keep your eyes open and look where you're going."

Penny's head tilted back, her feet ceased to move.

"In other words—stop boring people to death with it. That's what you're trying to say, isn't it?" she asked, her eyes looking directly into his.

"That's it. Be the old Pen, who could have a good time in the middle of the Sahara Desert. Your sense of humor has been your charm, Penny, don't lose it."

"Thanks, Davy. I won't."

The music stopped and she walked lightly beside him across the floor. Her eyes sparkled and when she reached the table she swished into her seat. "I'm back," she announced. Then she leaned her elbow on the table, cupped her chin in the palm of her hand, and said enigmatically to Carrol: "Do you know, I've kind of missed myself."

★

CHAPTER III

A CHANGED WORLD

When Penny came back to her everyday world, she came back as she always did, with gusto.

"Good morning, Uncle Lang," she called from the breakfast room door on Saturday morning. "Isn't it a gorgeous day?"

"Beautiful." Mr. Houghton looked up from his newspaper, and asked as he laid it beside his plate: "What are you and Carrol up to this morning?"

"We're going shopping. Mums gave me a super-sized check and we've planned to dazzle a couple of gents tonight." She slid into her chair, offered Perkins a joyous good morning, and added: "Of course, they're only David and Terry, but we thought we might inveigle you into an evening's frolic. Just to lend distinction to the affair, you know." She unfolded her napkin and coaxed over a spoonful of grapefruit: "Come on, Uncle Lang, and play with us."

"I?" Langdon Houghton laughed even as he shook his head. "How could I compete with two handsome young men?" he asked.

41

"Why, Daddy darling, by being handsomer than either one of them." Carrol's arms slid around his neck and she brushed her cheek against his. "By being handsomer, much more dashing, and I hate to sound mercenary, pet, by being much, much richer."

"Oh, so that's it." Her father drew her around to the arm of his chair, smiled at her fondly. "I'm invited to pay the check."

"You are. We always go to such expensively beautiful places when you're with us."

She laughed, gave his shoulders a tight squeeze, and winced when she felt how thin they were under the rough tweed of his coat. There were faint shadows beneath his eyes and she smoothed away a frown as she leaned toward him. "Please, Daddy, come with us," she begged.

"All right, honey. I'll take you all to dinner and then, afterward, I'll skip out."

"Thanks, darling." Her head turned at a step in the hall and her face lighted up. "Good morning, Cadet Parrish," she welcomed.

David came into the breakfast room wearing a dressing gown of Mr. Houghton's above his cadet trousers, a white scarf knotted about his throat.

"Morning, everybody." He bestowed a light pat on a brown head and a blond as he went around the table and smiled at the older man. "What's the news this morning, Uncle Lang?" he asked.

"Nothing very different, except that the Russians seem to have the Germans on the run. Are you joining the orgy of spending?"

"Not I." David shook his head emphatically. "Carrol and Penny can wear themselves out and I'll take the bodies to lunch. If they revive enough to stagger on afterward, I'll browse around in a bookshop."

"You might do your Christmas shopping," Penny suggested.

"Not this early in the month. I'll wait a couple of weeks." David attacked his breakfast and Carrol looked at him anxiously.

"But you *will* meet us at the Plaza for tea?"

He nodded a promise and she carried the thought with her through the day. I'll see him at noon, she planned, while Penny surrounded herself with bright dresses, and it won't be long until tea time. She counted the hours and Penny counted the costs.

"Two new dresses, a hat, and shoes," Penny enumerated that evening, giving her boxes to Perkins. "I should be a knock-out tonight."

They told her she was, but in her role of the new Penny, she was unconscious of it. She met Terry's sallies with quick laughter-provoking retorts, and her face above a red wool frock was serenely happy. "Isn't it wonderful to have such a good time?" she exclaimed, looking around the table at dinner. "I wish life could go on and on just like this."

43

"Well, not forever." David winked at Carrol, a tender, intimate little wink. "I'd like to get out of the Point before I have to walk with a cane."

"And of course, there's my ca . . ." Penny checked herself with an embarrassed laugh, substituting instead, "After all, it might get boring."

"It might, but I'd like to see you always as happy as you are tonight—all of you." Langdon Houghton's eyes rested an instant longer on his daughter than on the others, then he stood up. "I must run along now," he said. "Have a good time but don't stay out too late."

"We'll walk to the elevator with you, Uncle Lang."

David and Carrol got up and Terry's eyes followed the three as they went through the crowded dining room. "David's a lucky guy," he told Penny.

Yes, Penny thought. David and Carrol knew so well what they wanted from life, and they went so quietly toward their goal. "Trudy said once that David always walked straight, even when he was little," she mused aloud. "She said that I . . ." Penny picked up her teaspoon, turning it end on end.

"What did she say about you? Nothing good, I'll bet." Terry leaned toward her and she laughed.

"She said I back-tracked."

"Well, you do. You've been nice then horrid, nice then horrid, ever since I've known you. You're nice

44

tonight," he added with a sly smile, "I hope you'll stay this way."

"I will." Penny made a face at him but she fulfilled his hope.

She even scintillated when she got home; when there was no one there to see but Carrol. She bustled about the room, pulled up the Venetian blind and adjusted the drapes. She was businesslike and thorough and Carrol sat on a chair watching her.

"Are you sure you feel all right?" she asked, when Penny had the window adjusted to her liking.

Penny turned out the dressing table lights and closed a drawer. "Why?" she asked, stretching her arms above her head.

"Because it's the first time I've ever known you not to hop into bed first and leave the window and the lights to me."

"It's because I've reformed." Penny dived for one of the twin beds and burrowed under the covers. "But not too much," she laughed. "You can still turn out the other lamps. I don't want to spoil you."

She liked the new character she had built around herself and exuded sweetness and light all through Sunday morning. "Here comes the Duchess," David said, when she sailed into the library after lunch, a bowl of red roses in her hands. "Have you been in the garden, your Grace?"

"Terry sent them to me." Penny set the roses on a table and surveyed them proudly. "And on *Sunday,* too."

"What's Sunday got to do with it?" David, comfortable on the divan, looked at her over the funnies he was reading. "Does Sunday make them extra special?"

"Well . . . no. But I never think of people buying anything on Sunday. But perhaps he bought them last night after he left us . . . you know, just casually dropped into a shop and ordered them." She adjusted a long stem, cupped the blossom that topped it in the palm of her hand. "It's fun to think about them, when they were chosen from thousands of other flowers, put in a box and started on their way to me. It makes them more mine."

She stepped back from the table, her head on one side, as she admired the roses possessively; and Carrol laid down her section of the paper.

"I know how you feel," she said, curling up comfortably in a deep chair. "When David sends me flowers they have a nice personal sort of from-me-to-you look."

"That's because they're from me." David flung his paper to the floor, grinned at her, and glowered at Penny. "You aren't getting ideas, are you?"

"No, my dear brother, I'm not getting ideas." Penny whirled across the rug and rumpled his hair.

"You said to have fun, and I'm having fun. In fact, I'm *loving* it." She left him abruptly, laughing at his disgruntled smoothing of his short curls, and danced toward the radio. Soft strains of music answered her flip of the switch and she stood listening to it. "Oh golly, I'm happy," she said softly. "I wish I could interpret music. I'd like to be a dancer and say almost everything I feel in rhythm. Wouldn't it be wonderful?"

"Not to me." David leaned over the side of the sofa to pick up his paper, rolled farther, and remained on his stomach, reading from the floor. "You get the darnedest ideas," he mumbled.

"Well, you could do your expressing lying down; Carrol could glide, and I could bounce. You know, like Mickey Rooney and Judy Garland hopped up and down on the tables and chairs in a picture they did? They were expressing excitement. That's the way I feel."

"How would you do it, Pen?" Carrol leaned back to watch something that would probably end in disaster, and Penny balanced herself on her toes. She rolled her eyes toward the recumbent form on the divan, then leaned down and removed her stout brogues.

"First," she explained, "I would soar lightly upward." She set herself in motion, crossed the room in three bounds, and in her rise against gravity, struck David squarely in the back. He clutched at the edge of the divan, she grabbed unsuccessfully at the back, and they tumbled to the floor in a heap.

"If you want expression, which is just another name for a good roughhouse," he said, pinning her arms beneath her, "you're going to get it."

"Now, David, I was going on to Carrol," Penny panted, kicking and squirming to release herself.

"You're going to stay right here and say 'chubby baby.'" He held her arms with one hand, pressed her cheeks with the other until her mouth was puckered between their roundness. "Say it!" he commanded.

"I won't." Penny tried to wriggle free, gasping and sputtering.

"Say it!" David's hand was a vise and she floundered once more, kicked desperately, then lay flat. She knew she was defeated and her lips were trying to form the words when David's hand let go. "Listen!" he commanded, raising his head. "What's that on the radio?"

The music had ceased in the middle of a bar. A man's voice filled the silence. "At dawn this morning," his words rang into the room, "the Japanese attacked Pearl Harbor!"

"Oh, no!" Penny crawled up to sit beside David and Carrol ran to the radio. "What does it mean?" she cried, looking down at it. "He's talking about ships and planes!"

"It means war."

"Oh, David, *no!*" She turned to him, puzzled and frightened. "It's only a hoax, isn't it, like that stunt of Orson Welles?"

"It's no hoax." He, too, got up and went to the radio and Penny was left sitting on the floor by herself.

War, she thought as the voice went on describing the horrors of that peaceful Sunday morning. With Daddy going—and David. She looked at the two side by side before the radio, and heard David saying:

"It's war, honey. The Japs have jumped the gun and I may have a job right now."

"Then you'd better get back to the Point, hadn't you?"

"Yes. I want to talk to Dad."

Penny reached for her shoes. "I'll go with you, David," she said. She wanted to be at home. She wanted to see her father, to sit close to him, to touch him. She wanted to see him light a cigarette and slip the matches back into his pocket, to hear his quick step on the stair. She wanted to hold his cap in her hands, and his pigskin gloves, and his shaving soap; all the things that were so closely his. The sunshine filtered through the windows just as brightly as it had a moment ago but now it held no warmth. The roses on the table were just as beautiful, just as red . . . Penny turned her head to look at them. Terry would go, too. Poor Terry, who was so cocky and so gay,

49

would become grim and commanding. She looked again at the blond heads bent above the radio, her heart tightening into a hard cold knot. David. David would fight with real guns and real planes. Tears sprang to her eyes and she got up from the floor to slip quietly up the stairs in search of Carrol's father.

"Uncle Lang," she said, seeing him in the upstairs hall, "did you hear what the radio said?"

"Yes, I've been listening, Penny."

"But you don't think it's true, do you?" She searched his face hopefully, asking him to still her fears as he had so many times in the past, but he only shook his head.

"It's bad business—but it's true. I was just going down to talk with David."

"He says he'll have to go back to the Point, and of course I'll go with him."

"Then Carrol and I will drive you up. I want to talk with your father and get a good sound opinion about the thing." He slipped his hand through her arm and said as he turned her back toward the stairway: "Don't be too upset, dear. While we all knew it was coming, we need to keep our heads."

"But I didn't know it, Uncle Lang." Penny stopped on the stairs. "I knew we were training men, of course, in case we have to fight Germany, but somehow I didn't think that David or Daddy would really have to go. Why, I know lots of officers who have gone to England or Russia or Egypt, just to *watch.*"

"They went as observers, Penny, so they could come back to teach us. Of course we hoped this wouldn't happen, but it has, and I only wish I could get in and do my bit. I want to ask your father about it."

"You, Uncle Lang? Oh, no! Why . . ." Penny floundered for words. Her whole world was falling to pieces. Up to now, war had failed to touch her life. West Point, for all its training of young cadets, was perhaps the most peaceful spot in the United States. It had its dances, its athletics, its gay crowd in the Boodlers, and its officers who led the daily life of professors in a college. If this year had brought more talk of bomb sights, the Armored Force or the Air Corps, Penny had thought of it as only a first classman's interest in his career. So she looked at Langdon Houghton, at the grim set of his mouth, at the anger in his eyes, and her words were stopped. "It *is* war, Uncle Lang," she whispered. "I'm beginning to understand."

"It's betrayal, Penny. Starkest, foulest betrayal." Then he led her down the stairs to the library.

"I want to do my bit, Dave," he said an hour later, before the fire in the Parrishs' living room. "I'm too old to try for a uniform but there must be something I can do in Washington."

"There will be." Colonel Parrish looked at the cigarette he was tapping against an ash tray. "And I want to do my bit, too. There are hundreds of men, reserve officers, who can handle this teaching job I have. I've been trained to fight. I need to be in there, fighting." He stubbed his cigarette out and looked directly across the room at his wife. "What do you think, Marjorie?"

Silence answered him. Only the crackle of the fire broke the breathless waiting as all eyes watched her face. What would she say, this little woman who laughed so freely, who was the gay confident of her two tall men? They saw her look around the circle, clasp her hands about her knees, lean forward. "We all want to share, Dave," she said simply. "But men, like you, and David, will play an important part. Of course you don't want to stay on here. I only hope you won't have to."

"You mean, Mums . . ." Penny jumped up to stand before her. "You mean you want them to go to war? Daddy and David?"

"Of course not, darling." Her mother reached out to put an arm around Penny's waist. "But there is nothing else we can do. This thing has come to us and we must face it."

"You're telling Daddy in a quiet way to ask for a transfer; that you're willing to break up our home here and not be with David until he graduates. That's what you're saying, aren't you?"

"Why, yes, I suppose I am, Penny."

"And you're telling David that it's all right for him to be in the thick of it, too."

"That's what I *must* tell him, dear—but there's no use being dramatic about it."

"I'm not being dramatic." Penny dropped down at her mother's feet and reached for her hand. "The only way I've ever learned anything," she said, staring into the flames, "about how to meet difficult things in life, I mean, is from watching you and Dad. If you say it's the thing to do, you can bet it's the thing to do. I don't mind saying that I'm plain scared and if I had my way I'd run off and stick my head down a hole like an ostrich."

"And I'm scared, too." Carrol's voice was very small as she sided with Penny. "You see, Aunt Marjorie, it's all so different now that war is actually here. You and Dad and Uncle Dave have been through one war, but we . . . Well, we don't know exactly how to behave."

"I suppose you don't." Mrs. Parrish smiled and smoothed Penny's chestnut curls. "So suppose we start by having some supper. Trudy left the usual Sunday night supply in the refrigerator."

"Do you mean we're going to *eat!*" Penny cried. "Just as if nothing had happened?"

"Of course we are. You'll find that life will go on very much as it always has, with all of us eating and sleeping and going about our business."

"Which reminds me, I have to go, Mums." David

53

had been very quiet as he listened to the conversation that went on around him. Now he stood up and beckoned to Carrol. "Come help me into my wrappings," he urged.

He bent over his mother for her usual comradely hug and grinned a salute to the two men. " 'Bye Uncle Lang. Dad. I'll be over around four tomorrow, Pen, so tell Trudy to have a cake in the box." He gave Carrol a start and the low murmur of their voices came back from the hall.

"This knocks our plans into a cocked hat, doesn't it?" he said, twisting his cap through his fingers.

"Must it, David?"

"Sure. It's no good, getting married in war time."

Carrol leaned against the wall and glanced into the living room. "Your mother and father did," she reminded him, "and they seem to have weathered it."

"They were married before we got into the last war," he answered with a sigh. "That made a difference." He gave her his cap to hold while he shrugged himself into his overcoat. When he had it securely buttoned against the cold he stood looking down at her. "I'm not afraid of the war," he said with assurance, "because nothing is going to happen to me. It's just not having you with me that's going to be tough."

"But David, I want to be with you." Her hand reached out to him but he only took his cap and grinned.

54

A CHANGED WORLD

"Someday you will," he answered. "After the war is over." Then cupping her face between his two hands, he looked deep into her eyes. "Chin up," he whispered. He waved again to the group around the fire and the door closed behind him.

Carrol stayed leaning against the wall. How could one day so change a life, she wondered in despair. Only this morning David had been reading the funnies and as she looked at him she had imagined another Sunday, less than a year away; perhaps in a small house or an apartment on an army post, with David's boots and spurs cocked comfortably on a new divan. Now it wasn't to be. A Japanese nation had greedily blown lives and hopes and dreams to bits. Like a great monster it had snatched David, and thousands of other Davids, from the girls they loved. Only Penny's voice in the kitchen roused her.

"Come out here, Carrol," Penny called. "I want to talk to you."

She went slowly along the hall and was surprised to see Penny, enveloped in one of Trudy's voluminous aprons, on her knees before the refrigerator.

"How about cold chicken and a salad?" Penny asked, looking up with her usual grin.

"That's all right, I guess. Shall I make coffee?" Carrol leaned her forehead against the white porcelain and closed her eyes to keep two tears from sliding down her cheeks. Her face was so white and drawn

55

that Penny slid the platter of chicken back onto a shelf and stood up.

"Did everything blow up?" she asked soberly.

Only a nod answered her and she reached out in quick sympathy. "It's going to be all right," she soothed. "Why goodness, the war will be over in no time. Perhaps we can lick the Japs before David has to go." She had never seen Carrol sob like this before.

She must be terribly in love with him, Penny thought miserably. Golly, I hope I never let myself in for anything like this.

CHAPTER IV

TRANSPLANTED LIVES

The safety that enclosed the Parrishs' small world remained like a high fence around a lovely garden. The only change in daily life was that Penny and her father raced each other for the morning paper, and that Mrs. Parrish's knitting needles held serviceable olive drab yarn instead of the soft rose wool of Tippy's sweater. Christmas left a tissue-paper-trail, and more red roses for Penny. January piled war news against the straining fence; but February tore the gate from its hinges. It tore it so suddenly, so ruthlessly, that after twenty-five years of careful growing, the roots of the Parrish family were dragged from the soil and whirled into space.

But they were strong roots. They had been so lovingly nurtured that no matter where the maelstrom tossed them, they would grow again. Mrs. Parrish had no doubt of it on that cold bleak afternoon when her husband ran up the stairs.

"Marjorie?" he called, taking the steps two at a time. "Where are you?"

"In our room, darling." She stuck her needle into a pair of corduroy slacks that were so hopelessly torn but so comfortably Bobby's, and looked up with a smile. "Take it easy," she added, listening to the jangle of spurs as Colonel Parrish hurried along the hall.

"I can't." There was a flash of uniform in the door, then he was across the room, his arms around her. "Oh, Marjorie, Marjorie dearest," he whispered into her hair, "I'm going to England."

"Oh," Bobby's slacks and her sewing basket spilled to the floor as he pulled her to her feet. "When, Dave?"

"Right away. Oh, Marjie, is it all right? Do you think it's the right thing to do?" He was so doubtful, so worried, that she answered gently:

"Of course it's right, dear. What will you do over there?"

"Three of us are to go as observers, and we'll be gone about six months. I won't be in the actual fighting, Marjie."

He looked at her with the same expression that Bobby always mustered when he promised he wouldn't skate if the ice were thin, and she laid her hand tenderly against his cheek. Something was wrong with her breathing and her heart had departed from her body, but she thought she could manage her voice.

"I think it's—it's thrilling," she said in tones that

to her own ears sounded far, far away. "It's exactly what you wanted to do and it puts an end to the teaching. How did you hear about it?"

"The Chief of Cavalry phoned me. Oh Marjie, do you think you can get along without me?"

"Not very well, but I'll make a stab at it." She reached up to kiss him, to explain into his bewildered worry, "You know perfectly well that while I'll miss you, I'm a very capable woman."

"Yes, I guess you are," he answered, relieved. "Although you certainly don't look it—or act it most of the time."

"That's camouflage, Colonel Parrish. I may be deceptively decorated on the outside but I'm sturdy as a rock underneath."

"Yes, I guess you are," he repeated, hugging her to him. "That's why I said I'd go, without waiting to talk it over with you."

"You knew you didn't need to. You know how we both feel."

"Then let's go downstairs and make plans. We have a hundred things to decide and they have to be decided quickly."

They were on the divan before the fire, their heads bent over a pad, Colonel Parrish's pencil scratching rapidly, when Penny came in.

"What's the conference?" she asked, taking off her

goloshes and coming to hold her hands out to the flames.

"What?" Her mother tapped her nail against her teeth then leaned closer to the notebook. "You'd better put down that both cars are to be made over to me," she said before she looked up. Then she announced in an absent-minded way, "Oh, Daddy's going to England."

"Well, my soul!" Penny whirled around and stared at them. "One would think you're making out a grocery list. England? Since when?"

"Since about an hour ago." Her father laid down the pad and moved even nearer to Mrs. Parrish. "Come squeeze into the plans," he invited Penny, pulling her down on his other side. "What do you think about it?"

"I'm thrilled—I guess." Penny blinked at him. "Or I will be. I'm sort of stunned right now. Start at the beginning so I can get the picture."

So Colonel Parrish started at the beginning. He started there three times before dinner. Once when David stamped in at four o'clock, once for Bobby, and once with an abbreviated sketch for Tippy who seemed more concerned for her own comfort.

"But where are we going to live?" Tippy asked, the only one of the family who had yet considered that question. "Do we just stay right here and wait for you to come back, Daddy?"

"Well . . ." The Parrishes looked at each other. The ones on the divan looked at those left over on the floor. Where *would* they stay? No one had thought of that.

"I suppose the new instructor will want our house," Mrs. Parrish broke the silence. "Of course, David stays where he is—but the rest of us might go out to Chicago and be with Gram."

"Oh *no*, Mums." Penny vetoed the suggestion with horror. "We couldn't squeeze into Gram's little apartment. And we certainly don't want to rent a house there—we don't know anybody. How about New York?"

"It's too expensive." Mrs. Parrish shook her head decidedly and Penny's heart sank. She could see her career departing like a gray ghost and she blew it a mental kiss. She sank lower into the divan and heard her father say:

"It's selfish of me to go now, before I have to. We can't take the children out of school, Marjorie. Let's call it off and see if something else won't open up in June."

"Nonsense." Mrs. Parrish looked at her small circle of encumbrances. She had no idea what she would do with them but there was no hesitation in her voice when she spoke. "This is your big chance, Dave," she declared. "It will give you prestige and advancement —and you're going to grab it. I'm sure that something perfectly fine will turn up for us, too. Why, maybe we can drive down to Florida," she offered, clutching at a spot that might appeal to them, to even one of them. "A new term is just starting, and Bobby and Tippy could go to school there, and Penny . . ."

"Is through school, darling." Penny took her words as if adding to a round robin and went on from there. "I've been wanting to tell you that for weeks, and now I can. No more school." The ghost of her career came back, it ran back, and she saluted it gayly before her eyes met David's in a wide stare. "Oh," she breathed under cover of the discussion her declaration had evoked, "maybe I could stay with Carrol."

David, in the sign language they had understood for years, nodded. Penny returned the nod and they exchanged a wink. Then he got up from the floor and announced abruptly, with no apparent interest in the future spot where the Parrish heads might rest:

"I've got a telephone call to make."

He stopped by the phone in the hall, reconsidered, and went upstairs to close the door to his mother's room. "Hello, Carrol," he said, after the operator had pushed in a plug on her switchboard. "Dad's going to England."

He stretched himself full length on his mother's bed, pressed the receiver to his ear and grinned at the ceiling while he talked and listened. Penny's head appeared in the door but he motioned her away, went on talking, and at last dropped the receiver back into the waiting black arms of its holder with a satisfied smile. Then he borrowed his father's hair brushes, whistled while he straightened his blouse, and before he had reached the bottom of the stairs was pleased to note that the telephone was ringing.

"I'll get it," he called, jumping the last three steps. As one familiar with the instrument he cleared his throat and spoke into its waiting silence. "Colonel Parrish's quarters," he said. And then in a voice loud enough to reach the living room: "Why, *Carrol!* How did you happen to call up, now of all times?"

The family, listening unashamedly, caught the word "England," and then David was in the door. "Uncle Lang wants to talk to you, Mums, and then to you, Dad," he informed his parents who were surprised that he could terminate a conversation with Carrol in so few minutes. He usurped the divan they had left and stretched himself out. "Okay," he remarked cryptically to Penny who was clutching the mantel in a state of suppressed excitement. "It's fixed. But it's fixed bigger and better than we thought."

"Sure?"

"Sure."

"What's fixed?" Tippy wanted to know. "Nothing's broken, and you and Penny talk so funny."

"We feel funny." Penny swept Tippy up and began waltzing her around the room. "We're an exciting

63

family," she exclaimed, adding an "ouch," as Tippy not only stepped on her foot but kicked her on her ankle. "I thought you had learned to dance."

"We don't dance fast like this at dancing school," Tippy panted. "And we count. I can't dance 'less I count."

"Well, Bobby can." Penny left Tippy in the middle of a one- two-step, and lunged for her younger brother. But Bobby, in twelve year old bashfulness, sat more firmly on the seat of his Boy Scout shorts and glared at her. "Nuts," he said. So she twirled herself to the hall archway and pressed against the casing. Now and then she nodded with delight, turned to grin at David whose head had come up over the arm of the divan, and at the click of the receiver had barely time to tuck her skirts decorously beneath her, and to stare musingly into the fire.

"Darlings, what do you think!" her mother cried from the doorway Penny had quitted but a moment before. "We have a home!"

"Where?" Penny, with Tippy and Bobby, were a chorus. And David sat up.

"Don't I get to talk to Carrol?" he asked.

"Not now—she's hung up." His mother cut him off and turned to Colonel Parrish. "Oh, Dave, isn't it wonderful?" she cried. Then she ran across the room and dropped down beside Penny. "Uncle Lang settled everything, just as he usually does," she explained, smiling at them all and feeling very much like a fairy godmother. "We're going to live at Gladstone Farms this winter," she rushed on, "and he and Carrol will come out for week-ends. Miss Turner, who has been perfectly miserable since Carrol hasn't needed a governess, and who has had no family since Carrol's grandmother died, will teach Tippy. Isn't it wonderful?" she repeated, pausing for breath. She caught Tippy by her fat legs, pulling her down onto her lap and asked as she hugged her, "Aren't you happy, baby?"

"Umhum." Tippy nodded her crown of curls but Bobby deepened his scowl and inched nearer.

"I'm not," he muttered. "It's sissy."

"But she isn't to teach you." Colonel Parrish put his hand in his pocket and brought out a cigarette. "Stand up, Bob," he said as he lighted it, "and let's see how tall you are."

"Yes, sir." Bobby scrambled to his feet, stretched until the top of his head was level with the cigarette, and at his father's nod of approval added another half-inch.

"Just about right," Dave Parrish decided, nodding to his wife. Then his eyes came back to the straining form before him and he asked: "What would you say to military school, Bob?"

"To military . . . Oh boy!" Bobby's young arms clawed at his father and Colonel Parrish dusted ashes out of the shock of hair that was pressed against his chest.

"Careful, son," he warned, "you'll set us both on fire and I won't get to England and you won't get to school."

"Yes, sir, no, sir—oh gee!" Bobby translated his happiness in a war dance that brought Trudy to the door.

"You can tell her what it's all about," David said struggling up from the couch. "As usual, I've got to get back. Give me a lift, Pen?"

"Delighted." Penny left the scene of mad revelry and said when they were in the car: "Dear Dad. It takes a load off his mind, doesn't it?"

"Umhum. It means so much for him to go but I really think he was on the verge of backing out. Uncle Lang's a peach."

"Well, he certainly thought fast." Penny skirted an icy spot in the road, and added: "It wasn't two minutes after you called Carrol until he was on the phone."

"And he even settled Bobby in that time. It'll do the kid good; knock some of the cockiness out of him."

Grant Hall was outlined in the headlight's glare and David reached for the door handle but Penny put on her brakes and laid her hand on his arm. "David," she asked soberly, "doesn't it make you feel badly to think that our tour here is over? That we've got to break up our home and not live here any more?"

"It's tough." He sat with his hand on the door, staring out into the dusk. "But if this is the worst thing we're going to have to face, Pen, I'll be grateful."

"I know. The next time Daddy goes, it may not be to just observe. And then, there's you . . . and Carrol . . ."

"Well, keep your chin up." David turned to push his fist against her cheek. "And keep Mums cheerful, remember that."

"I will, Davy."

"Okay. So long."

"So long." Penny watched him spring across the shallow steps of Grant Hall before she started the car. "Oh me," she sighed, easing out from the icy curb, "I kind of wish I had a crystal ball."

★

CHAPTER V

A Gladstone Welcome

Quarters 48 had become just any house again. Boxes stood in the hall, furniture that had fitted in so comfortably, stood on the snowy lawn looking discouraged and dispossessed. Moving men were rough with it as they hoisted it into vans and carted it off to storage. Even the sign on the front steps had no meaning, for Lieutenant Colonel D. G. Parrish was gone.

Yesterday he had been there; weighing his luggage on the bathroom scales, choosing, discarding, losing everything he touched, joking and planning for his trip. Now . . . Somewhere on the wide Atlantic a bomber was winging its way. . . .

"Well, in West Point lingo, we had three years and a butt of a swell detail," Penny consoled herself as she helped Yates wedge a suitcase into the Houghton station wagon. She climbed across Tippy's doll house to reach for a portable radio that Michael was holding up to her. "Goodness," she grinned as she took it, "we're going to look just like the Okies."

"Even the Okies ate." Dick Ford, sitting in the snow

69

on a trunk locker, was supposedly half of the two-man detail David had brought over with him. But while the others worked his assistance consisted of spurring them on. If a trunk were to be brought downstairs he was safely in the basement; when the garden tools were discovered behind the furnace and rushed to the moving van, he had quietly migrated to a safer region. He conserved his energy by explaining to the others how they could best expend theirs. Now he sat on the trunk locker and thought about his appetite. "Doesn't Trudy even have a cake?" he grumbled. "She always has a cake."

"Go ask her." Penny, caught between the back seat and a mountain of clothes on hangers, called to his already departing back, "and if she has, bring us a piece. No, wait a minute." She perched the radio atop a pile of boxes and leaned out. "How much more have we, Mike?"

"Just the trunk."

"Then we'll go in and forage, too. I've saved a corner up in front and Yates will pitch it in."

Michael helped her down and as they went through the garage to the side door he looked at her and grinned. "I think you kind of like it, Pen."

"Like what, moving? I adore it." Penny pushed the door open, shoved a pile of excelsior aside, and led the way into the kitchen.

Trudy was bent above a box that held kitchen

utensils, and Dick, with a slice of cake already on its way to his mouth, was insisting that if she turned the lid of the roaster over she could squeeze in another frying pan.

"Law, Mr. Dick, you gets me so con-*fused*." Trudy brandished the disputed lid at him and removed her cake box from the sink to the top of the refrigerator. "You ain't grown up none since you was at Fort Arden. How do you think you're goin' to fight an enemy with all your nonsense? They's jes' goin' to laugh at you."

"Well, that's all right. While they're laughing I'll take 'em prisoners." Dick wiped the cake crumbs from his mouth and Trudy chuckled.

"What's more like it is, you'll be settin' down restin' yourself an' they'll take you prisoner. Want a piece of cake, Miss Penny, honey?"

"We're all starving, Trudy." Penny reached for the cake tin while Michael deftly fitted the roaster, lid and all, into a corner that both Dick and Trudy had overlooked.

"There you are," he said. His white teeth flashed in his lean dark face at Dick's disgruntled look and he held his piece of cake away from a reaching hand. "You've had your share," he admonished, ruffling Dick's red mop. "What's become of Carrol and David?"

"They're packing the stuff Dad left behind so it

71

won't worry Mums." Penny found a cracked plate in the wastebasket, washed it and covered it with three wedges of cake. "As soon as this box goes out we're ready," she sighed. "Mums will come back tomorrow with Yates to clean up, and then the Quartermaster will check us out."

"I'm going to be pretty lonesome around four o'clock every afternoon," Michael told her. "We've had some swell times here." He offered the remains of his cake to Dick and caught her hand. "Let's take a last tour," he suggested, "for old time's sake."

She walked with him through the deserted rooms, their shoes echoing on the bare floors. "I'm going to miss you, Penny," he said, leaning against the living room wall and looking down at her, "miss always knowing that you're right here, I mean."

"We have had good times, Mike," she answered thoughtfully. "Ever since we were kids and had 'the crowd.' We were such a swell crowd."

"And even when we went in a gang I always considered you my drag. You knew that, didn't you?"

"I suppose so." Penny, too, leaned against the wall and her eyes began to dance with hidden laughter.

"What's so funny?"

"I was thinking about the night of the horse show, when I was fourteen. I had on a new dress with a taffeta petticoat that rustled, and I thought I looked lovely. Someone, I think it was Dick, began teasing me and calling me a glamour girl. And it made David mad so you asked me to go have a coke. My heart was beating a thousand throbs to the minute and I was frightened. I wanted to go, but you didn't seem—just Mike. I was suddenly conscious of you as a boy." Penny looked up at him and smiled. "The hardest thing I ever did," she said with a shake of her head, "was to get up out of that chair and go with you."

"I remember it, too. That was when I first began to notice you. And I've noticed you ever since." Michael met her eyes but there was no answering smile on his lips. "Have you felt that way about me, Penny?"

"Oh, Mike." She looked across the room into the cold gray ashes of the fireplace, wondering, honestly, how much she had thought of Michael in these four years. He had made so many of her week ends gay. He had been so loyal, so devoted—so *always there*. At last she turned back to him. "I love you almost as much as I do David," she told him.

"That's a hard answer to give a guy." And she could see the muscles tighten along his jaw.

"Why? When I love David so much?"

"Being told you love me like a brother. It's been said before, Pen."

"Maybe. But then I really mean it, you know." Penny laughed shakily and Michael's smile came back.

73

"Well, anyway," he said, "being loved like a brother, or a brother's roommate, is better than not being loved at all—providing you don't stop."

"You know I won't. I couldn't if I wanted to." Penny's tone was sincere and he traced the outline of her nose with his finger.

"Next week end, hm?" he asked.

"I'd love it if the family finances will stretch to a room at the hotel." She gave herself a push from the wall and frowned. "How awful it's going to be," she said, "to have to pay to stay at West Point. Goodness, I hadn't thought of that."

There was a clatter on the stairs, a bump, and laughter, and Michael went into the hall. David and Carrol were on either end of a large cardboard carton and Carrol was sitting on the step.

"I dropped my end," she explained through the banisters.

"I'll get it." Michael bounded up the stairs and Penny stood at the foot.

Dick sauntered in from the kitchen, his jaws moving rhythmically while he surveyed the scene. "If you'll just stand her up on end," he suggested, "she'll go better. Sort of pull. . . ."

"Oh, pipe down." Michael moved the box for Carrol to slide around. "You haven't lifted a finger all afternoon," he grumbled, "and you'll go back to barracks and boast about how tired you are."

A GLADSTONE WELCOME

"Why, Mike Drayton, you wouldn't be as far along as you are if I hadn't been here to run things." Dick's grin was complacent and he lifted his round face above the newel post. "Mrs. Parrish," he called upward, "we're all set now."

"Coming down," her voice answered. "If someone will ask Trudy to collect Tippy from next door." Then her face appeared above the rail. "It seems queer not to have to hunt for Bobby," she said, "but I must say it's been easier. I hope the poor little thing is all right."

"He's happy." David lifted his end of the carton and nodded up to her. "The thrill of his uniform will keep him from being homesick. Let's go, Mike."

He backed carefully down the steps and Dick reached out a lazy hand to open the door for him.

"Put it in the little car," Penny called, going to the coat closet for hats and coats. "Mums will take the big one with Trudy and Tip and the dog. Carrol, you get all the mess in the station wagon, and I'll bring up the rear with the left-overs."

She sorted out the wraps, fumed impatiently at delays, and tooted her horn loudly when she saw the big car go out the driveway. "The Okies are off," she shouted through the window to the three who stood watching. "All we need is a feather bed tied on top." She nudged Carrol's car with her bumper, blew her horn in a last blast and shifted her gears. Her red

75

mitten signaled, her tires crunched on the ice, and she swept down the drive and into the street.

The caravan proceeded slowly along the highway because of icy ruts the snow plow had failed to dislodge, and Penny released a tired sigh when she saw her mother go through the lodge gates of Gladstone Farms. She remembered the first time she had driven through them with Carrol; when she had mistaken the small caretaker's cottage for the mansion that waited magnificently on the end of the winding drive. Lights gleamed now behind its tall windows; and set high on a terrace, its long wings topped by turrets it reared against the sky like a castle. Penny swept into the semi-circular drive behind the others in time to see a servant throw open the great front door. Once she had been awed by this grandeur; now she hopped from the car and ran to Mr. Houghton who was hurrying out.

"Uncle Lang," she cried, throwing her arms around his neck, "you're a perfect angel!"

"It was the Good Fairy again," he whispered. "She's taken care of us for almost four years and it looks as if she'll have a lifetime job." He dislodged her with a pat and ran down the steps. "Hello, Marjorie," he said, throwing open the car door and holding out both hands. "Welcome home."

And it seemed like home to her—as nearly as any place could be home, without a tall officer and a shock-headed boy. She had a glimpse of Miss Turner, smiling and faded in the drawing room, of Tippy climbing the wide staircase beside Trudy, of Carrol and Penny on their knees in the library trying to introduce a doubtful police dog to a disdainful collie.

"It's so good to be here, Lang," she said gratefully, giving her coat to Gerald, who, as Perkins' son, had taken his father's place in the country. "I can't ever thank you enough."

"You mustn't try. As Penny used to say, 'we're a family.' Families don't need to thank each other—they know."

"Of course they do. But I wanted to say it just once." She walked with him into the drawing room but stopped before a portrait of a young girl that hung over the marble mantel. "You knew Carrol's mother, didn't you?" she asked Miss Turner, taking the delicate blue-veined hand in hers. "I never come into this room without feeling her presence."

"She was a lovely person." Miss Turner too looked at the portrait and added softly: "Carrol is very like her."

"Except for her atrocious taste in dogs." Mr. Houghton's eyes twinkled as Carrol backed into the room dragging the collie by his collar. "What's wrong with Marmaduke?"

"He won't be pleasant to Woofy." Carrol let go of

77

the collar and the collie sat down, staring haughtily over his white shirt front. "Woofy wagged his tail and wanted to be friends but Duke snarled at him."

"That's because he's jealous," her father answered. "He'll get over it. What has become of Penny?"

"She's on the phone listening to a perfect flow of cajolery. Terry Hayes called her."

"Oh dear, is he in New York again?" Mrs. Parrish looked disturbed and Carrol answered quickly:

"No, he's down at Dix, and pining away from what I could hear. Penny seems to think it a huge joke that will cost the Lieutenant several dollars unless he can convince her quickly that she should come to New York for a date Saturday. She keeps repeating that . . ." Carrol turned her head at a voice from the door.

"Come here a minute," Penny motioned, wagging a beckoning finger. "I need advice."

She rushed Carrol up the stairs and when they were in the rose bedroom they shared closed the door. "Listen," she said, collapsing on a chaise longue, "what am I supposed to do? I have a date with Mike for Saturday night."

"Then tell Terry so, and make him believe it."

"But you don't understand yet. You don't know what he's offering." Penny ran her fingers through her hair and sat up. "Janice Ware is opening in a new play Saturday night—and he has tickets for it!"

A GLADSTONE WELCOME

"Oh Allah, Penny! That *is* hard." Carrol pushed Penny's feet over and sat down suddenly, herself.

"Yes sir, Janice Ware—the actress of my dreams, the gal I met once, the gal who took me to dinner. I've waited three years for her to come back from Hollywood. And now at last, she's here and . . ."

"Surely, Pen, Michael would understand."

"I don't know." Penny threw herself back into the pillows again and her hair stood wildly upright. "I suppose Mike *would* understand," she groaned, "but I can't give Terry Hayes the satisfaction of knowing I broke a date for him."

"But if you make him know that it's just to see Janice Ware . . ."

"He knows I can see her any other night. She's sure to be a hit."

"Well then, I don't know what to tell you. What do you want to do?"

"I don't know." Penny pulled a pillow from behind her, pleating the ruffle absently before she tossed it on the floor. "Mike was so sweet this afternoon . . ."

"And it was nice of Terry to get the tickets because he knows how you adore Janice Ware."

"Yes. I told him about it once . . . the day he made me so mad." Penny leaned back dreamily. "It was kind of sweet of him at that," she meditated aloud. "It's the first thoughtful thing I've ever known him to do."

"Except load you down with roses. Do you think you'll go?"

"Carrol, I can't—there's Mike. It's a definite date."

She sighed and looked so disconsolate that Carrol tried to find a solution. "Why don't you think it over tonight?" she suggested. "Then talk to David about it. He might put it up to Mike in such a way . . ."

"Oh, do you suppose he *could*?" Penny sat up again, hope revived. "Shall I call him now?"

"No, wait. It's his supper hour. You know that Terry isn't going to turn back his tickets this early, so we can drive up to West Point tomorrow when your mother goes."

She talked away Penny's impatience with sound advice and added, as Penny got up to comb her hair, "Besides, I'm like Mr. Micawber—I always hope that something will turn up."

★

CHAPTER VI

BRIGHT STAR SHINING

Penny sat in the darkened theatre, her eyes on the curtain. Any moment now its great folds would part. Slowly at first, just a crack, a teasing glimpse. Perhaps a room; perhaps a garden. And then, faster than the eye could behold the wonders it disclosed, it would sweep open, unveiling fairyland. What would it be? And when would a burst of applause herald the entrance of Janice Ware? Penny leaned forward clutching her purse in cold hands. The footlights glowed, the curtain began to sway ... She thought she couldn't bear it.

Terry Hayes beside her watched her face instead of the stage. He knew now why she had broken her date with Michael Drayton, and instead of feeling the triumph that had possessed him during dinner he shared a kindred loss with him. Penny had no date with either one of them. Twice he leaned toward her during the play; once to catch her gloves that slid unnoticed from her lap, and once to say during the third act: "It's a hit, Penny."

"I knew it would be." She forgot to answer him un
til they were on their way up the aisle. "Even withou
all the curtain calls and the remarks people made dur
ing intermissions, I knew it would be a hit. Janice
Ware could make any play a hit."

"Not always." Terry signaled a cab and said as he
put her into it, "The best of actors can't have succes
without a good playwright."

"No, that's true." Penny agreed with him reluc
tantly then leaned back in a corner of the taxi. "Bu
Music on the Mountain was written for Janice Ware
"Oh, Terry," she sighed, "do you suppose I can eve
do it?"

"I wish I weren't so sure of it."

"But how do I start? I don't know where, or how
to begin."

"Well first, if I were you," Terry saw Fifth Ave
nue before them and leaned forward to speak to
the chauffeur. "Drive through the park," he said, and
then again to Penny: "Why don't you write Miss
Ware a note, asking her if she'll let you talk to her
You've met her and she might remember you."

"Oh, do you think I'd dare?" Penny sat up straight
her face glowing with the light he had magically
turned on. "Oh, Terry, you're wonderful!"

"I'm a fool. I should tell you it is utterly impossible
for you to be a star, that it's the worst life you could
choose, that you'll never be any good as an actress . .

But instead of that," he reached for her hand and patted it, "I lessen my chances of a photo-finish by politely letting you have the inside of the track."

"And it's sweet of you, Terry." Penny laid her other hand over his. "You really are a pretty nice guy," she said.

"Because I told you something you should have thought of for yourself?"

"No, because I think you understand how I feel. Listen." She was so excited and eager that she drew her feet up under her and slid around on the leather seat to face him. "You know how you've always sketched horses and polo games and hunts, and sold them to magazines? That's a creative urge, isn't it?"

"Yes."

"And it doesn't mean that you aren't satisfied with your career in the army. You just have to release something. Well, that's the way it is with me—only I can't have two careers at the same time."

"You could if you'd choose something else, writing for instance. You said once that you wanted to write."

"But not enough. I wrote a poem once." Penny smiled, thinking of the poem. "It was all about Time with a capital T. It said, as nearly as I can remember, 'Oh Time, thou squandered one, unvalued by mankind, I see thee flitting while I sit—and fain would break the chains that bind me in submissive nothingness, to race with thee!' It was terrific. It suffered

83

for two pages and the teacher read it aloud in class and said I had 'possibilities.' Possibilities, Terry, think of it! When it was my whole soul spread out on paper."

There was no answer so she sat looking at him, at his head turned toward the park, away from her. Poor Terry. She had stolen the center of his stage. Not only that, she had left him in the wings all evening. Penny was contrite. She tried to throw him a quick cue by saying in a polite-little-girl-tone of voice: "It was sweet of you to take me to the play, Terry."

And then he looked at her. "Sweet?" he said with a wry smile. "It was a darn-fool thing to do. But it told me what I wanted to know. You're all right, Penny, and you'll make the grade. And you'll not only make it, but I'll be behind pushing or out in front pulling for you, all the way."

"Why, Terry!"

Her eyes were wide with surprise. It was as if a small clay figure had suddenly walked off its pedestal and had grown into a man. Why, it's as odd as "man bites dog," she thought. It's something people ought to know about. But all she could say was: "And I haven't bored you?"

"Bored me? Good heavens, Pen, you're the first girl I ever knew who had something on her mind beside clothes and lipstick and a line of patter. You may do a lot of things to me in the future but you've never bored me in either the past or the present."

"Oh, I'm so glad." Penny leaned back against the cushions with a sigh of relief. "You looked out the window so long," she said, "I thought your feelings were hurt."

"I was getting a new picture of you and wondering how I could give you a new one of me."

"You have."

"Then let's forget the bad start we got off to. I'm not the show-off you think I am, or the sappy kid who got out of West Point much too young for his job. Will you try to believe that, Pen?"

"Of course, I will." She answered him promptly, but even in the dull glow of the cab she knew it would be hard. His cap still sat at an individual slant, as army caps are never supposed to do, and while the words he continued to pour out were in praise of her—they built him to the sky.

"You could almost sell me the Brooklyn Bridge," she said, when he told her good night at the Houghtons' apartment door. But once inside she stood thoughtfully in the hall. "Now, I wonder if he could?" she debated, discarding her promise to believe him. "It might be that Mr. Terry has done some more very smart scene stealing. I seem to remember that the conversation swung to the confidence I must have in him, to his nobility, his sudden mental coming of age. Well. . . ." She shrugged her shoulders. "It really doesn't matter, if he's happier this way."

GLORY BE!

She peeked into the library to see if Mr. Houghton
were still up and finding the room empty, turned out a
trail of lights as she went upstairs. It was strange not
to have Carrol in the other bed, to know that she was
dancing at West Point. Doing all the things I should
be enjoying, Penny thought, slipping off her coat and
sitting down to stare at the wall. Her red fox jacket, a
Christmas gift from Mr. Houghton and the pride of
her heart, trailed forgotten on the floor beside her hat.
Now and then she recrossed her knees, and at last she
got up and went to Carrol's desk. At one o'clock her
pen was scratching busily; at two she was reading the
result of her labors, and at three she was crawling into
bed, weary-eyed, but satisfied with the note she would
send to Miss Janice Ware by special messenger.

She sank into dreamless slumber that lasted until
ten o'clock when the ringing of the telephone sent her
hand groping toward the bedside table.

"Um," she said when Carrol's voice asked if she
were all right. And, "Umhum," she yawned when
Carrol asked if the play had been a hit. Then, at the
mention of the play, she woke up. Struggling upright,
she blinked back the sleep, and began a word for word
description of the dialogue.

"That's enough," Carrol interrupted before Penny
had done justice to the first act. "I'm telephoning
from the hotel and it's costing me by the minute. It
will be cheaper to see the play. We're going to skate in

the gym this afternoon and I only wanted to ask if
you'll come up. Faith and Denise are here."

"Oh, golly." Penny flopped down again. "I might
get an answer to my note," she parried. "Miss Ware
might want to see me any minute . . ."

"Have you sent it, yet?" The inquiring voice on the
other end of the line was so knowing that Penny was
forced to add weakly:

"No, not yet, but I've written it."

"Then don't be silly. You may wait days for an
answer. Have Daddy or Parker drive you up."

"But what will I do with Terry?" Penny's voice rose
to a wail. "He doesn't have to go back to Dix until
tonight and I've got him again this afternoon. Shall I
bring him, too?"

"I'm sure Mike would love it." Carrol's voice was
flat but Penny hoped she detected a giggle.

"I'll ditch him someway," she promised. "After all,
even if he did suggest my writing to Miss Ware, he
isn't as nice as Mike."

"Of course not. See you at the gym."

There was a click and Penny was left holding a life-
less medium of thought transference. "I couldn't bear
to wait too long," she sighed to it, forgetting her problem of Terry and Michael. "Maybe just today and
tomorrow."

But she did wait. She not only waited, but she managed to control her impatience in the nine days that

elapsed before Perkins brought her a square blue envelope.

"It's come, Carrol!" she called, stumbling up the stairs, her eyes on the angular handwriting. "I'm afraid to open it."

Carrol met her in the hall. "Let's take it in the sitting room," she cried, catching Penny by the arm and guiding her like a sleepwalker.

She put her on a divan, waiting in a fever of impatience while Penny continued to turn the envelope over and over in her hands. "Here, you open it," Penny said at last. "I haven't the courage."

She dropped the letter and shut her eyes with a prayer when she heard the crackle of the flap being torn and the stiff rustle of paper. Then she laid her head weakly against Carrol's shoulder and dared a peek at the open page.

"Whe-e!" she cried, before Carrol could begin to read. "I see something. Give it to me. Look! She says 'dinner on Wednesday—matinee.' . . . Oh boy, oh boy, oh boy!" She jumped up, waving the letter. "I'm so excited I think I'm going to burst!"

"Well, sit down and read it, then burst. I'm excited too, but I'm curious." Carrol reached out to pull her down again but Penny flopped onto the divan, panting.

"She says," Penny began, her hands trembling un-

til the words were blurred, "she says, 'Dear Penny':
Isn't it wonderful to think she calls me that? And that
she actually *wrote* this?" Penny's eyes caressed the
note and she gulped with ecstasy.

"It is. But why don't you go on? Why prolong the
agony?"

"Because it's fun. It makes it last longer." Penny
grinned, then took a deep breath and began again.
" *'I was so happy to have your note, for indeed I have
thought of you, and have wondered, often, if you were
any nearer your goal. Perhaps we can talk things over
if you will come to the Wednesday matinee and will
dine with me at Hardy's, as you did before. A ticket
will be at the box office and I shall look forward to
seeing you. Very sincerely, Janice Ware.'* Look at it,"
Penny pointed. "Her autograph—right there for everyone to see!"

"And of course you'll be there before the doors
open."

"I will if I don't faint on the way." Penny still
stared at the signature then she looked up with a sigh.
"I'll be a wreck by Wednesday."

"It's only until tomorrow."

"It *is?* Oh goodness, I'll never be ready in time."
Penny was startled into action. "I've got my clothes
to think of and my hair . . . oh dear, I must telephone
Mums, or maybe I should run out there . . . and then,
there's Terry . . ."

"What about Terry? You aren't taking *him* with you, are you?"

"Well, I should say not! But I promised him I'd let him know how things came out, if I got an answer, that is, so perhaps I'd better call him, too."

"The truth of the matter is that you want to call everyone you can think of." Carrol laughed, and at Penny's sheepish grin, added: "Well, hop to the phone and spread the glad tidings to Faith and Denise. They'll be far more responsive than Terry."

"All right. But first, what do you think I should wear? I had on a new suit the other time and I want to look just as nice now."

"Why, your green wool and your red fox jacket and the little fox hat with the green wing. It's the most stunning outfit you have."

"And the only complete one." Penny, that matter decided for her by Carrol and a clothes allowance, spent the rest of the morning on the telephone.

"Let's all drive up to Gladstone," she said at lunch to Carrol, Faith and Denise, when Perkins was re trieving her napkin from the floor, proffering her a clean fork, and mopping up a puddle of ice water. "I'm in such a twitchet I drop everything I touch."

"I think we'd better." Carrol turned to the two who had rushed over to be a part of the excitement, the chorus that surrounded Penny's stellar role. "Ever the wear and tear on tires is better than the damage to our nervous systems if we stay caged up here with her all afternoon. Let's spend the night," she suggested, "and get her back just in time for the matinee."

Marjorie Parrish was as happy for her child's good fortune as were the three who were carefully assisting Penny from the car. "It's wonderful, dear," she said, standing on the wind-swept terrace and holding out her arms. "You see, things are working out for you."

"They are if we can keep her from breaking a leg." Denise ran up the steps, laughing.

"She's terrible, Mrs. Parrish," Faith added, "really she is. She runs into things and goops."

"So we brought her up to you." Carrol gave her Aunt Marjorie a kiss and hustled Penny inside. "We hope you can calm her."

"I think I can." Mrs. Parrish winked before she looked gravely at Penny. "I do wish Daddy could know about this," she said softly.

"Oh, I do too!" Penny's eyes were dark pools of tenderness. "Daddy would be so pleased. I wish we could send him a cable—but I don't suppose it would ever reach him." She sat down, looking soberly at her mother, and the others looked at her too, but they laughed.

"There, you see?" Mrs. Parrish smiled and gave Penny a hug. "All you have to do is start her off on another track. Keep the switches open and you can guide her any place you want today. She's hypnotized."

"I am not." Penny laughed with the others but she admitted that she did feel lightheaded. She ate very little dinner and at bedtime submitted passively to the ministrations of three self-appointed maids.

"Don't you think I should have some cold cream on my face?" she asked, under the hair brush that Faith was plowing through her mane to the rhythmic count of a hundred.

"You never have had." Carrol poised her manicure scissors over one of Penny's nails, nipping the cuticle carefully. "But you can try it if you like. Run get some from Aunt Marjorie, Denise."

"And I really should have Trudy brush my shoes." Penny sat up in bed, grinning at the circle that admired her. "I don't know whether I'm ready to go to sleep or out for the evening," she giggled. She looked down at her hands that, covered with lotion, were now incased in white kid gloves, and felt her head in a flowered scarf tied over knobby curlers. Her face was greasy, and vaseline dripped from her eyelashes. "I think I'll get up and wash," she announced.

"You will not." Six hands pushed her back and Carrol scolded; "We've wasted a whole evening on you and if you don't show results by morning we're going to write letters to the companies, telling them their junk is no good."

"All right." She lay down again but when the house was quiet, when Carrol's regular breathing told that

she was asleep in the next bed, Penny slipped softly
out and down the stairs. She collected objects from
about the house, and for some moments was very
busy. Then she returned silently to her nest, slid under
the covers and lay down on her back.

When early morning sunlight streamed in the windows, Carrol turned over, gasped, and raised herself
on one elbow to stare at the sight in the other bed.
Penny lay just as she had last seen her—but her face
was scrubbed clean, her hands were incased in Mr.
Houghton's goloshes, and a tin mixing bowl covered
her head.

★

CHAPTER VII

A FALLING STAR

"Oh dear, oh dear," Penny thought, standing in the
alley by the stage door, clutching her hat and pressing
her wrists against her hair to keep it from blowing
straight out in the wind. "Here I go. I hope I stop
trembling." She reached for an iron handle on the
door, gave it a quick tug and ducked inside.

The old doorman, sitting beside a call-board,
dropped the front legs of his chair to the floor and
looked at her over a copy of *Variety*. "Lookin' for
someone?" he inquired.

"Yes; Miss Ware. She's—she's expecting me."

"Right down the hall and to the left," he pointed.
Then he returned to his paper and missed the smile
Penny sent him.

He was old, very old; and long ago had lost his
dream of becoming a second Richard Mansfield, but
he belonged inside the theatre and Penny envied him.
"Do you mind if I wait here a minute while I comb
my hair?" she asked. "The wind blew me to bits."

"Why not?" He turned a page and Penny took off

95

her hat and ran her pocket comb through the tangles. When she was ready, when she was sure the seams of her stockings were straight and had put on her gloves, she smiled again, murmured a "thank you" to the magazine, and went into the dark corridor. Her heels tapped on the worn boards and she tried to walk lightly. When she reached the door that had a large star painted on it she lifted her hand, then dropped it. She could hear voices from behind the door and she waited, wondering if she should knock or let the present visitor emerge. While she stood, indecisive and hesitant, a young man came along the corridor. He was definitely coming to Miss Ware's dressing room and in desperation Penny's knuckles cracked sharply against the wood.

"Want to see Janice?" he asked, flinging open the door. "So do I. Go on in."

He stepped back for her and said over her shoulder: "It's okay about the change of lighting, Jan. Just thought I'd let you know."

"Thanks, Martin." The woman at the mirror turned and Penny's heart pounded so loudly she thought someone was beating a drum. There was Janice Ware, titian-haired, lovely, unchanged! And she was holding out her hands, smiling. "Why, Penny Parrish," she said in her throaty voice that could carry to the highest balcony, "you've grown up. Come here and let me look at you."

She turned to the room's other occupant, a man who was crouched on a sofa with a script held close to near-sighted eyes, and asked: "Isn't that a wonderful name for an ingénue, Jake? Penny Parrish?" Then she laughed and said to Penny with a shake of her bright head: "He's my manager but I shan't introduce him. He's reading a new play; won't hear a word until he's finished. Come tell me about yourself."

So Penny sat down in a deep, pink chair and began stringing sentences together, carefully, as a child strings beads on a cord. But Janice Ware said, "England? How facinating." And as she dusted powder on her nose, asked, "And David—it is David, isn't it? Where is he?"

She was doing things to her face as she listened and Penny forgot about the sentences and launched into a glowing account of David and Carrol.

"You're just as entertaining as ever," Miss Ware said when Penny paused for breath. "Look, darling, run down the corridor and find Felice, the same maid I had before, while I bring Jake out of his stupor. Then you and I'll pop across the street and have some dinner. Right?"

"Right." Penny bustled along the hall importantly. She, too, had business here now, and she found Felice and brought her back. Then before she knew it, she and Miss Ware were in Hardy's, sitting at the same table where they had sat three years ago.

"I never dared hope I'd be doing this again," she said happily, laying down her soup spoon and smiling across a low bowl of flowers. "I've practically lived on the memory of the other time."

"And you still want to be an actress?"

"More than anything in the world." Penny forgot her soup. She rested her hands on the table's edge and leaned forward. This was her chance. "It's something I *have* to do," she began. "I know you understand what I mean."

"Yes, I do, Penny."

"It just seems that . . ." She looked into space, searching for words, for the right words. "As if nothing else in life is so important. Of course I might not be very good," she admitted haltingly, "But I do feel that I will, if only I can get a start . . ." The words she had found, that were coming so easily, died in her throat. She stared across the room.

"What is it, dear?" Miss Ware turned her head, her eyes following Penny's, and she saw a young officer bowing to them from a wall table. "Is he someone you know?" she asked. "He's frightfully good-looking and he seems to be coming over."

"Yes, I know him." Penny picked up her spoon again. Then she looked up at the face smiling delightedly down at her. "Miss Ware," she said woodenly, "may I present Lieutenant Hayes?"

A FALLING STAR

"It's a nice surprise, finding you here," Terry said after he had acknowledged his introduction to a famous actress with all the formality it deserved. "It was lonely down at Dix so I thought I'd dash up for the evening."

He turned from Penny's unresponsive stare to add, engagingly naïve: "The army doesn't go in for bright lights, Miss Ware."

"I can imagine it doesn't." She saw frank yearning in his eyes and motioned to the vacant chair that held their purses. "Won't you sit with us?" she invited cordially, thinking of him as a friend of Penny's.

"May I?" Terry's smile flashed out and Penny, watching the waiter lay another place, took her purse from him and knew that her chance was over.

The charm was turned on now, and she watched Terry vying with a professional for the center of the stage. Theirs was a battle of wits, of small talk, arguments; and Penny ate her dinner quietly like a well-bred child listening to her elders. She thought her watch had stopped, but when she held it to her ear it was ticking as stolidly as her heart. Her only comfort was that this couldn't last forever.

"Good-by, Penny, darling," Miss Ware said at the entrance to the theatre. "Good-by, Lieutenant Hayes. This has been a wonderful interlude between performances and I do want to finish the argument with you about taking in the refugees. I'm sure I could con-

vince you if I didn't have to run." She put out her
hand to both of them but Terry held it longer.

"Until Sunday afternoon," he said, before she took
it away.

Then she was gone and Penny, with no need for
further pretense, was running through the theatre-
goers who crowded Forty-fifth Street.

"Penny! Wait a minute!"

Terry's long stride was pounding behind her but she
dodged a group of people and turned onto Broadway.
She prayed for a cruising cab, a bus, a streetcar, anything, but the crowd on the corner caught her, wedged
her fast.

"Penny!" Terry's hand slid through her arm and
she made no effort to escape.

"All right," she said, her eyes cold as she looked
up at him. "You've done all the damage you can—
now what do you want?"

"I want to take you home. I want to talk to you."

"There's nothing you can say."

Crowds pushed her, the endless crowds that would
walk up and down the street until midnight. She was
jabbed by rough elbows; felt her hat go off, saw
Terry reach for it, heard him say:

"We've got to move on, Penny. Let me get a cab."

"No. This is the only place I can find where you
can't hurt me. When you leave—I'll go." She braced
her feet as an irate voice growled in her ear:

"Listen, lady—why don't you walk wid de rest of us? You're blockin' traffic."

"Penny," Terry gave the man a shove, walled him off from her, "can't you see that I was interested, that I was trying to help you? Didn't she ask us to come to tea on Sunday?"

"She asked you to come to tea." Penny closed her eyes with pain as a sharp heel crushed down on her instep. "What I do," she said between stiff lips, "is no concern of yours. I hate you, Terry Hayes, as I've never hated any human being in my life before." Then she jerked away from him, dodged through a hole in the strollers, and was lost in the moving mass.

She was hardly conscious of walking the long blocks home. Her feet moved automatically. Long blocks across town; with lighted restaurant windows where lobsters lay on ice in red magnificence, where turtles swam an endless marathon in tanks; short blocks up-town, where Florida fashions bloomed behind ice-incrusted window panes; where small dogs trotted, pulling at their leashes; cars, an endless stream of cars; and once, a voice that warned, "watch your step, lady." Apartment houses opened their doors to flow-ing skirts and bulky overcoats; a cigarette glowed on the pavement in short-lived splendor. Penny trudged on wearily, hatless, her arms crossed in the sleeves of her jacket to shut out the cold.

"Good evening, Miss Parrish." The doorman

whisked her inside. He was smiling and snug in his layers of uniform and stout boots. The foyer felt hot after the icy wind; steam hissed from a radiator her feet tingled. Then the elevator was shooting up—eight, fourteen, twenty-two—soon it would reach twenty-eight. The doors would open soundlessly and richly, and she would be home. Perhaps not home she thought with a sigh, because she had no home now. But safe inside, and warm, with people who loved her.

"Why, Penny!" Carrol heard the doors, quiet as they were, and was running across the wide hall. "What happened to you, darling?"

"Nothing—just nothing." Penny tugged at her gloves. "I walked home," she explained dully.

"But where's your hat?"

"Why . . ." Penny's hand reached to her hair. "I guess—Terry must have it."

"Oh, Penny." Carrol took her jacket from her drooping shoulders with a sigh. "He showed up, didn't he—at Hardy's?"

"Umhum." Penny nodded then looked down at her instep. "I got stepped on," she said, bending down to look at the bruise as if it were the only catastrophe of her evening. "It hurts like fury."

"In more ways than one." Carrol tossed the jacket onto a chair and called into the library: "Daddy, Penny's back."

"She is?" Langdon Houghton laid down his book and crossed the room. "How did it go, Pen?" he began. Then he saw her disheveled hair, her torn stocking, and her eyes that seemed too big for her face. "Why, Penny, child," he said, holding out his arms. "Come here to your Uncle Lang."

Her lip trembled but he pressed her head against him, stroking her tangled hair. "There, there," he soothed, "why, you're as cold as ice. Carrol will ring for some hot tea and . . . oh, little Penny, everything will be all right."

"I know it." Her voice was muffled in his coat and over her head his eyes sought Carrol's.

"It was Terry," she whispered.

He nodded, then pressed his lips together. "Listen, dear," he said, tipping up Penny's chin and looking down at her. "You must forget tonight, whatever happened, because you're going to have your career. Believe that, Penny."

"Yes, Uncle Lang, but . . ."

"Let's have no 'buts.' Things may not always go smoothly but you'll win out, Penny. Don't you remember the Good Fairy that you made up when you were a little girl? Hasn't she always helped us in a pinch?" He smiled at her and saw her struggle with an answering smile. "Trust the Good Fairy," he said, "or me—or your own determination." Then he gave her a pat and added: "Now, run along with Carrol.

GLORY BE!

Make the tea yourselves and talk this out while you're doing it. Feel better now?"

"Much, Uncle Lang."

"Then run along." He watched her go through the dining room with Carrol, sighed, shook his head, and went to answer the telephone.

"Yes," he said, replying to a question that followed his "hello," "Penny is safely home."

A metallic voice came through the receiver, hurried, almost incoherent; and as he listened, Langdon Houghton felt the tension easing from his mouth. But when he spoke his words were clipped and brief.

"Penny is quite upset, Lieutenant Hayes," he said. "And I believe—at least just now—there is nothing further you could say to her. Good night."

Then he heard Carrol and Penny in the dining room and went to help them with the trays they carried.

★

CHAPTER VIII

PENNY PROTÉGÉ

Penny lay on the divan in Carrol's sitting room at Gladstone, staring at the wall. She could see Trudy bustling about in the bedroom, and from Trudy's straight back she knew a lecture was coming. At last Trudy could bear it no longer. She closed a drawer softly and came to stand in the door.

"What do you think you're doin', Miss Penny?" she asked, folding her hands on her apron in a characteristic pose.

"I'm knitting." Penny still stared into space and Trudy clicked her tongue.

"Tch, tch," she began. "There you is . . ."

"Well, I'm knitting my brows." Penny forestalled her. She swung one knee over the other and looked around as Trudy chuckled.

"Miss Penny, honey," she said, "why didn't you make some of those snappy come-backs the night you was havin' dinner with Miss Ware an' Lieutenant Hayes? Why'd you jes' sit there all froze up inside?"

105

"*Just sit there!* Well for goodness' sake!" Penny flopped over onto her stomach to stare incredulously. "What chance did I have to do anything else?"

"You had as much chance as they had. You was invited to the party. You're jus' as good-lookin' and jus' as smart as that young lieutenant. From what your mamma told me you must have looked awful dumb."

"Well, I did—but there wasn't anything I could do about it."

"There was plenty you could've done. I can't see that it was so awful for Mr. Terry to plump hisself down with you. He's a personable young man and you's a personable young lady. An' it could kind of showed Miss Ware that you was popular an' bright."

"But they didn't talk to me."

"Did you talk to them?"

"No." Penny was honest in her answer. "I couldn't think of anything to say."

"Pshaw. You could have thought of plenty. But no, you was jes' like Tippy when Bobby takes her candy." Trudy came to stand beside the divan. "You jes' looked all big-eyed and awful pitiful. Now, didn't you?"

"Yes, I guess I did." Penny blushed hotly at the picture she must have made, sitting like a school girl, primly and miserably straight on her chair. She looked up at the sternness of Trudy and stammered: "I—I guess I wasn't so smart."

"No, you wasn't." Trudy laid her hand on the brown head that had burrowed into a pillow. "You knows," she said earnestly "that if a friend of Miss Ware's had come along, you'd have been sparkly and talked right up. But it was your friend who was spoilin' things, an' you was mad. I ain't proud of you, Miss Penny, an' I don't think your mamma is, neither."

"Mums? Why, Trudy, what did she say?" Penny sat up with a bounce.

"Nothin' much. She jes' sighed an' shook her head. 'Poor Penny,' she said, kind of low, 'she thinks she's so grown up when she's such a little girl. I do hope, for her sake, Miss Ware won't lose interest in her.'"

"Oh goodness, I hadn't thought of it that way." Penny clasped her hands together and looked up, her eyes imploring. "You don't think I've messed it up hopelessly, do you?"

"Course not." Satisfied, Trudy turned back to the bedroom but Penny jumped up and followed her.

"I can see now," she said to Trudy's back that was bending over a drawer again, "that Miss Ware would have enjoyed a chat more than listening to my silly ambitions. But I wanted to get everything out in one fell swoop."

"You got to take time an' build things up."

"But Terry confused me so . . ."

"You got to keep your head an' turn mishaps into advantages." Trudy straightened slips, changed lingerie from one drawer to another, but Penny persisted.

"He always acts so important."

"That's cause he feels important. He ain't actin'. He's jes' doin' what he wants to do, and most of the time folks enjoy it. You two is so much alike that when you gets together sparks start flyin' an' someone always gets hurt." Trudy turned around and warned with a shake of her head, "You be seein', honey, next Sunday, that it ain't you."

"Thanks, Trudy, I will. I had decided not to go to Miss Ware's on Sunday, but now I think I will. Oh, Trudy," she reached out and hugged her mentor's narrow shoulders, "what would I ever do without you?"

"That's what I'm always awonderin'." Trudy freed herself to lay her work-worn hand on Penny's arm. "You's awful wobbly, honey. You go skitin' in all directions like a little girl on roller skates that can't stand up on 'em. I don't know what you're goin' to do when you won't have your mamma and your papa and Mr. David and Miss Carrol an' Mr. Houghton an' me to hold onto. You need such a lot of bolsterin'."

"Maybe I'll grow up." Penny's eyes were solemn but Trudy smiled.

"Maybe you will," she admitted. "You've been tellin' me that, every time I scold you, since you was little. I reckon that some day it will happen, but I'll

kind of miss you like you is. Now run along. Jes'
lookin' for somethin' to do in this house keeps me so
busy I ain't got time to do it when I finds it."

Penny went downstairs, and some strange shyness
kept her from hunting up her mother. I made such a
commotion about meeting Miss Ware, she thought,
abjectly humble now, that I'd better prove I can make
something of it instead of explaining why I muffed my
chances. She played the piano for an hour, in a painstaking but discordant murder of *Star Dust*, and when
she heard Gerald's fourth and weary insistence to the
Fort Dix operator that Miss Penny was not in and
might never be in, surprised him by taking the phone
herself.

"Hello, Terry," she said blithely, "sorry I missed
your other calls." Then she smiled because her new
frontal attack had left the great Hayes speechless.

"I- ah- have called you several times," he said at last.
"I just wanted to know if you're all right and if you
got your hat."

"Oh, I got it, thanks." Penny chuckled silently.
"That was a cute little box it came in, and the orchid
was divine. I never had an orchid before, Terry, and
I'm saving it for Sunday."

"And that's another thing I wanted to say. Good
luck on Sunday, Pen. I'm terribly sorry about the other
night."

"Don't be. I acted like an idiot." Penny took a deep

breath and plunged in, wholeheartedly honest. "There wasn't any reason why you shouldn't show up at Hardy's."

"I was just so darned interested, Pen. I tried to keep away, but I couldn't. You aren't mad at me then?"

"Of course not. And please forget some of the things I said until I can apologize properly on Sunday."

There was a wait for cricket-chirps and popguns that a telephone likes to imitate, before Terry's voice said through them: "I don't believe I can make it Sunday. Some work came up . . ."

"Don't be silly." Penny wriggled with joy at the halting explanation. "Of course you can make it. You have to see me in my first orchid."

She sat at the desk drawing cartoons that were as ridiculous as her conversation until Terry announced he had no more change to feed the coin box. Then she returned so vigorously to her annihilation of *Star Dust* that her mother wondered from upstairs if she were planning complete destruction of the piano too.

The family suffered with her through a rollicking Friday and Saturday and as the result of her boundless energy, welcomed Sunday afternoon with naps and peaceful quiet. The shadows grew long, fat sparrows turned into brown pompons under the eaves, and Trudy had led a sleepy Tippy to bed before Penny's tires crunched on the gravel.

"Yoo-hoo," she called, running through the hall and hurling herself on her mother who was nearest. "I'm a protégé!"

Without waiting for an answer she flung a grin at Mr. Houghton and at Carrol who hovered over Mrs. Parrish's shoulder. "Yes sir," she announced, "You are now looking at Miss Penelope Parrish, protégé of Miss Janice Ware! Oh boy!"

"Good gracious, Penny, what are you talking about?" Her mother extricated herself and Penny flung her hat in the air for Carrol to catch. "It sounds exciting—but what does it mean?"

"It means . . . Oh darlings, it means everything!" Penny ran from one to the other, dropping kisses where they fell. Then she swirled into a chair and caught her breath. "I feel as if I'd drunk gallons of coffee," she said, "had been caught in a hurricane, done a parachute jump from a plane, ridden a . . ."

"In plain words you feel excited." Carrol chose a footstool before the fire and nodded. "We know. So start at the beginning and we'll arrive at the protégé part with a build up. Let's go."

"Okay." Penny collected herself and took a deep breath. The three who watched her knew from past experience that prodding would only waste time, so they sat patiently waiting. "Well first, I got there—to Miss Ware's apartment. I was so nervous I could hardly park the car but with the help of the doorman and a very nice man who was passing, I made it. Then I went upstairs and thought I'd faint before I could ring the bell. I was sure Terry would be there, quite comfortable and very much at home, but Miss Ware came to the door by herself. I mean she came to the living room door after a maid had . . ."

"Taken your coat. We know. Go on." Carrol nodded and Penny jumped up.

"Let me show you how Miss Ware greeted me," she cried. "It will give you a better picture of us." She held out her hands to her mother, arranged her face into a mask of happy surprise, and swayed across the room in what she, at least, considered a glide. "Oh, Penny, dear," she murmured into her mother's amused stare, "I'm so glad you came early."

Then she dropped her hands and shrugged. "I didn't know I was early," she said candidly. "But before I could be embarrassed, Miss Ware said . . ." Penny took only one hand this time and used it to propel her mother across the room. "I'm so happy to have you," her voice became unconsciously throaty and she smiled fondly, "because I want to tell you how busily I have planned for you since I saw you last." A chair blocked their forward progress and Penny pointed to it. "You can sit there," she directed, "because we sat down on a little sofa and for quite a while I didn't do much talking. That was when she asked me to be her protégé."

"How did she ask you?" Langdon Houghton's eyes twinkled. "Can you act that for us, too?"

"No, I don't think so." Penny shook her head. "I can't remember everything exactly."

She struggled to sort out the speeches, to relive her afternoon, and Carrol thought: it doesn't matter how entertaining she is to us, she doesn't know she's cute and funny. This is the day she's lived for and she was never more serious in her life. She sent a smile to Penny who answered it by saying:

"Then Miss Ware asked if I could do some acting for her, Shakespeare or something; and I thought about *The Philadelphia Story*. You know, Carrol," she reminded, "I saw the play four times and the movie six and worked out one scene by myself, so I thought I could be Katharine Hepburn if I could be anybody. Well, up I got and away I went. Miss Ware watched me, all interested, except once, when she looked over my head and smiled and nodded. I could feel that someone was standing behind me, and was going to stop, but she said, 'go on, Penny, it's only Lieutenant Hayes.' Only Lieutenant Hayes! Golly, it was hard to go on."

"What did Terry do?"

"Well, believe it or not," Penny grinned at Carrol, "he said, 'that was swell, Pen.' And Miss Ware said, 'Why, dear, it was *splendid*. I have great hopes for you.'"

"Did she really say that?" Her mother forgot her amusement and leaned forward, too.

"Yep, she did." Penny nodded solemnly. "And after she had greeted Terry, very casually I might add, she said, 'you won't mind if Penny and I talk business, will you?'"

"Did he mind?"

"Uncle Lang, he actually listened. And he had a good long time to do it in." She awoke to the fact that she had been standing like a lecturer on his dais and looked about for a chair. "This is the exciting part," she said, sitting down and crossing her knees. And again her voice became rich, her gestures controlled. "Miss Ware said, 'Penny, I've thought about you a great deal and it seems foolish for you to waste the rest of this year going to dramatic school. So I talked to a dear friend of mine who was a famous actress in her day. She is quite old now but she still takes a few pupils whom she thinks have promise. I talked with her about you and she has agreed to coach you.' Right there I nearly died. But before I could faint or pass out or anything, Miss Ware went on. 'It would mean a lesson every day, Penny, and while it would be expensive, dramatic school would cost as much.' Oh Mums," Penny looked at Mrs. Parrish and asked, prayerfully: "*Could* we do it?"

"I think so." Her mother nodded, but added: "What did you tell her?"

"Well, I thought I'd pretend I could even if I had to call her up after I got home, so I said I'd love to do it. The woman sounded so wonderful because she has played with every actor who is famous."

"What is her name, honey?"

"Well," for the first time Penny looked dubious. "It's kind of disappointing," she said. "I thought it would be Violet Haversham or something like Dame Whitty, but . . ." She shook her head and added sadly: "It's just Emma Jones."

"Emma Jones." Mr. Houghton's smile, sent to revive her, was reminiscent. "She was the toast of New York when I was a boy. We used to watch her drive up Fifth Avenue in her carriage and I always thought she was the most beautiful woman I had ever seen, and the most divine actress. Penny, you're truly in luck."

"Am I?" Penny's face beamed. Then she threw herself out of the chair, landed at her mother's feet, and clutched her around the knees. "The hard part's coming now, Mummy," she said, reaching up to put her arms around her mother's waist. "Miss Ware has a stock company over in Connecticut and she wants to send me there this summer."

"Oh, Penny."

"Of course, darling, I won't go if you don't want me to." Penny caressed her mother's cheek, but added persuasively: "I know you'll want to talk it over with

Dad—but couldn't we just *pretend* I'm going to until he gets home?"

Mrs. Parrish looked down at the eager face tilted to hers. Her hope that Penny would forget her dream of the stage died in that moment. Penny was so sure of herself; as sure as David in his West Point training. Children do grow up, she thought, and we can't hope to keep them with us. But she only asked quietly:

"What do they do in the stock company?"

"They do everything." Penny sat down on the floor to launch into her explanation. "They have a barn that's made into a theatre, and they paint scenery and make costumes and do a new play every week. Of course, they have a director and a couple of good actors who get paid. But the rest of us," she looked up to say, "just get our expenses. Would that matter?"

"That would be the least of it. What else would you do?"

"Well, we rehearse one play while we're putting on another, and everyone has to take a turn at all kinds of parts. Then Miss Ware comes up for one week and takes the lead in a play. Wouldn't it be wonderful if I could get a part that week and be on the stage with her?"

"Yes, I suppose from your viewpoint it would." Mrs. Parrish realized that Penny, although unaware of it, was using the present tense and including herself in the company, and she sighed. "What do you think, Lang?" she asked. "I'm so bewildered."

The man who had been a second father to Penny looked thoughtful. "I know, Marjorie, that you're wondering what Dave would answer," he said. "It's hard for me to advise you. But thinking of Dave too, I believe he would know that Penny will never be happy until she tries her wings a little. She may not care for it as much as she thinks she will . . ."

"But I will, Uncle Lang. If Mummy decides to let me do it, we'll have to face that fact." Penny crossed her feet under her and looked at Carrol. "You know that, don't you?"

"Yes, that's true." Carrol answered quietly for she was as sure as Penny. "I've known what she thinks, Aunt Marjorie; probably better than any of you, except David. It's all she's talked about for years. I think it would be easier for you to decide if you thought you were only letting her have a little fling, but . . ." she gestured helplessly, "but I'm afraid you're deciding her life for her."

"Then that's for Penny to do." Mrs. Parrish tried to smile through a sigh. "She'll have to work it out, even if she knows it's a hard road to travel."

"And I can be a protégé?" Penny was on her knees again, facing her mother.

"Oh, I suppose so." Mrs. Parrish's consent was reluctant, but once she had it Penny clutched it like a spent swimmer dragging a water-logged body by the hair of its head. She had seen her career going down for the third time in a whirlpool of argument, and after its astounding rescue she hurried to apply first aid. "You're all witnesses!" she cried. "I'm to have a chance at making good."

"Oh, we'll back you up." Carrol came to sit on the arm of Mrs. Parrish's chair. "I wouldn't worry too much, Aunt Marjorie," she whispered, loud enough for Penny to hear. "There's always Mr. Micawber's hope that something will turn up."

"And a lot of good that would do now," Penny answered saucily. "I'm firmly launched."

"Oh yes?" Carrol stood up, poised for flight before she added: "And what about the guy who sent you the orchid?"

"Why, you deceitful, two-faced fiend!" Penny scrambled to her feet but Carrol was through the door and streaking for the stairs.

"Hey, wait," Penny called. "I forgot to tell you. The orchid guy has been made a captain!"

★

CHAPTER IX

AN AMATEUR VILLAIN

"Don't you think it would be nice to have a promotion party for Terry?" Mr. Houghton suggested a few days later when he and Carrol were walking their horses across the rolling fields of Gladstone. "Penny has been cooped up in town, working like fury, while we've been out here basking in the good country air."

"It would be fun." Carrol dropped the reins on Floridian's glossy brown neck and let her hurry to match the long stride of Scamps Lad. "David and Michael have week ends; and while Mike is going to visit his aunt, I know he would rather come here. I hadn't asked them because . . ." She looked anxiously at her father. He rode his big horse with an easy swing, but a lazy tour of the estate contented him now, when a year ago Scamps Lad would have filled his morning and both Martinette and a polo pony would have been thoroughly exercised by mid-afternoon. They spent more time at Gladstone than they had in previous winters; and although he said it was because the Parrishes made it so pleasant, Carrol no-

119

ticed that he rested a great deal and took very little
interest in his business. Sensing her scrutiny, he turned
his head and she hurried to finish her sentence. "I
didn't know if Penny would be out. She's in such a
fog."

"Marjorie says she'll be here. And you might call
Faith and Denise if you think you can get dates for
them."

"Well, there's always Dick, but I doubt if Bob
Prescott could make it, not being a first classman. I'll
see what I can do."

She urged Floridian forward as Scamps Lad broke
into a canter but her eyes were still on her father's
face. It looked so pale. "Do you feel all right, Daddy?"
she asked when they turned their horses over to a
groom at the stable.

"I feel swell. But I'm tired," he admitted. He looked
at the long lane leading to the house and added. "Let's
be sissies and drive up."

She would have dismissed his suggestion for a party
had he not reminded her of it after lunch. "Call up
your crowd," he urged, "and have Penny bring Perkins and a maid with her. We need some pep around
here." He took his newspaper and his magazines
from a table and went off down the hall, calling:
"Tippy, are you beating me to our naps?"

Carrol turned to a window and stood looking out.
"Do you think he's well, Aunt Marjorie?" she asked,

her eyes on the bleak February day that stamped its icy signature on the patient brown grass. Then she turned so quickly that Mrs. Parrish, caught off guard, could only answer hurriedly:

"Why Carrol, I take naps too, you know. I'm always pretending I'm very busy in my room, but truthfully, I'm secretly sleeping."

"But you only nap. While Daddy—oh, Aunt Marjorie, I've seen him. He lies there, so still, so white and tired, that nothing wakes him. He's exhausted."

"Then nature is helping him, building up his reserve strength."

"But you don't think he's well, do you?" Carrol asked the question so bluntly that Mrs. Parrish shook her head.

"No, dear, I don't think he's well," she said, slipping her arm around the slender shoulders. "But just how ill he is, I don't know—and it seems he doesn't want us to know. So don't you think it would be kinder to pretend we don't notice any change?"

"But he should see a doctor."

"He has, Carrol. That much I do know because he told your Uncle Dave so. He had a thorough check-up at the Mayo's when he went West last fall. They say he needs a great deal of rest."

"Oh. Well, if he's seen a doctor," Carrol squared her shoulders, "we'll go on with the party."

She called Faith and Denise, received enthusiastic

acceptances from David and Michael, and the fervent hope from Dick that he could get a pass. When Penny called for her bed time chat she surprised Carrol by screaming into the phone:

"Who do you think I saw today?"

"I couldn't guess."

"Then I'll give you a hint." Penny loaded the wire with adjectives and Carrol could imagine the gestures that accompanied them. "We used to know her at Fort Arden when she was a brat; but now she is a gorgeous creature, but gorgeous, with clouds of floating black hair and eyelashes that twine and twine . . ."

"Not Louise Frazier!"

"Louise in person, pet, and looking too Park Avenue for words; in spite of the fact she has a job."

"I'm completely stunned. What's she doing?"

"Publicity for a vedy, vedy expensive cosmetic firm, dear," Penny mimicked. "Isn't it a riot? She wanted to know all about the Fort Arden gang and I detected a blush when she asked about David. So I spread it on with a spatula—all about your beautiful romance, his love and devotion . . ."

"Oh, Penny, you didn't!"

There were giggles on the other end of the line. "I did, so help me. I let her know that David is gone for good. And then I had an inspiration."

"What? Although I'm afraid to hear it."

"I'm going to give her Terry! Won't they make a

wonderful couple? Now if I can just get them together."

"Penny, you're incorrigible. Poor Terry." Then,
pitying him, she was reminded. "We're having a promotion party for him Saturday night. Will you bring
up a pair of sterling silver captain's bars?"

"Sure. And may I bring Louise? It will be a show
that comes once in a lifetime and you know you want
a ringside seat."

"All right, bring her—or tell her to come along
later. I want you to come Friday evening if you can."

"I'll be there, because poor dear Miss Turner is
getting awfully tired of chaperoning me. Now run
tell the family the news."

Carrol laughed when she told them. She laughed,
but she shook her head. "I know just how it will end,"
she said, "and it's going to be terrific."

"How?" her father asked curiously.

"I can't tell you—but Penny is in for a big surprise."

She was still smiling when Penny arrived on Friday
night. "She's coming," Penny snickered, "and Terry's
coming, and they both want to spend the night.
Louise remembers Terry from our hero-worshiping
days but he can't place her and that simply burns
her up."

"Did you tell her, Pen?"

"Sure I told her. And I could just see her weaving
her eyelashes into a spider's web to ensnare him."

Carrol had a mental photograph of Louise turned vampire and wondered what had happened to her since she had seen her last. She knew from past experience that Louise was daring, unfaithful to any friendship, selfish and calculating; but to have become as devastating as Penny described her, she must have concentrated on glamour and technique. Her surprise on Saturday afternoon was great, however, when Parker opened the car door for a young lady who was dressed in a severely tailored black suit; who wore no make-up, and looked very shy and sweet.

"Well, she was done up in silver fox when I saw her," Penny mumbled as Louise came up the steps to them. "I think she's a chameleon or an actress— maybe she should be the protégé."

Whatever she was, Louise knew the part she was playing, which was that of an army girl having a simple week end in the country. She was charming to Mrs. Parrish, chatting about her own mother and father, and eager to hear of Colonel Parrish and the children. And Penny was nonplussed.

She'll revert to type when David comes, and Terry, Penny promised herself. But she didn't. She greeted David with a friendly hand clasp that included Carrol as she said: "I think it's wonderful about you two, David. I envy you from the bottom of my heart."

"Thanks, Louise." David smiled and reminded her,

"It's been a long time since we've had the whole gang together."

"Yes, hasn't it?" Then she walked away, leaving David where he wanted to be, alone with Carrol.

"How did she get here?" he asked.

"Penny found her. She has some idea that Terry will fall for her like a ton of brick."

"Does she want him to?"

"She says she does." They both turned to watch Penny who was running to the door, calling out into the cold:

"Come in, my Captain, oh my Captain. You certainly are late to your own house party."

"Couldn't help it. I got hung on the Major's coat tails." Terry ran up the steps and took her face between his cold hands. "Got a kiss for Daddy?"

"Don't be ridiculous." Penny pushed his hands away, then seeing Louise going through the hall, hung on his arm and said sweetly: "Oh, Terry, darling, I'm so happy, now you've come." That will set her in motion, since she's sure David is beyond reach, Penny thought.

But Terry was looking down at her strangely. "What's the matter with you?" he asked. "Why the sudden collapse?"

"Because it's nice to have you," she insisted. Then she gave him a dig with her elbow and whispered,

"That's Louise. If you don't remember her, pretend you do."

"Oh, that's it. You want her to think you have a heavy suitor." Terry nodded and allowed himself to be led along the hall. But when he saw Louise halfway up the stairs he bounded up after her, exclaiming: "Why, it's Louise Frazier, by all that's holy. When did you grow up?"

Louise regarded him coolly. "You're Terry Hayes, aren't you?" she murmured doubtfully. And then at his nod she held out her hand and smiled. "It's nice seeing you again."

"Then come downstairs and tell me so." He backed down a step trying to draw her with him, but she only shook her head.

"Sorry," she said. "I have to change."

Penny, watching from below, rushed into the drawing room to nod at Carrol. "It's going fine," she gloated. "She'll take him off my hands in no time."

But she was wrong. Faith and Denise arrived; Michael and Dick, with Creighton Page, a brother first classman. Luggage was distributed in various rooms, and those who were spending the night dressed in a minimum of time and rushed downstairs again. But the door to Louise's room remained closed.

"This is the way Carrol should have it oftener," Mr. Houghton said to Miss Turner who sat on a divan beside him. Her gentle faded eyes were watching the bright dresses mingled with the uniforms and she held Tippy's hand.

"Look, Miss Turner," Tippy lisped through her missing front tooth, "that's Louise Frazier coming down the stairs. She's an awful skunk."

"Why, Tippy! That isn't a polite way to speak of anyone."

"But she is—Bobby said so. Isn't she a skunk, Uncle Lang?" Tippy edged over to stand between Mr. Houghton's knees and he drew her back against him.

"I wouldn't say that," he smiled over her curly head that leaned against his chest. "She's a very attractive girl." He looked at Louise in her long red dress; high at the neck, long-sleeved, its severity relieved by a heavy gold chain. She's almost as old as David, he thought, and has infinitely more sophistication than any of them. I wonder if poor little Penny has made a mistake?

Louise came into the room quietly, almost shyly, and Dick was the first to see her. "Well, look who's here!" he cried. Heads turned as Dick, who had been her slave when they were younger, staged for her the perfect entrance.

She seemed content to stop beside his homely grin, but Penny toured her around the room, making elaborate introductions and displaying her proudly. When

they went in to dinner Louise was carefully placed between Terry and Michael and Penny cast hopeful
glances across the flowers and candles.

A watched pot never boils," David said to her in
an undertone when she became exasperated with
Louise for enjoying her soup more than the sallies of
Michael; and with Terry who was shooting black
scowls over the table instead of the bread pellets he
was suggestively rolling.

"But I invited her here for a purpose," Penny insisted. "She hasn't any right to let me down."

"Well, give her time." David turned back to Carrol
and Penny devoted herself to Creighton Page and the
curbing of her impatience.

But it was no better after dinner. Louise stood by
the fireplace drinking her coffee and talking to Dick.
"Oh, I suppose I'm enjoying it," she answered his
blunt remark that she looked bored to death. "But I
am rather tired of people. One meets so many in New
York."

"Yes, I've heard that quite a few live there." Dick
rested his elbow on the mantel and swung one foot
across the other. "I suppose you're very busy socially,"
he baited.

"I go out. And of course I have my work. The people I know are so much older than all of you." Louise's
long lashes flicked upward as Terry passed on his way

to Penny. "Take Terry Hayes, for instance," she illus-
trated. "When I was sixteen I thought he was so old
and so wonderful. Now," she shrugged her shoulders
and lifted her cup, "I find that he hasn't grown up at
all—that he's even sillier and younger than the rest
of you."

"That's almost a compliment in these trying times."
Dick was unusually serious. "David thinks he's old
enough to get married, and we all think we're old
enough to lick the Japs and the Germans." He rubbed
his stubby red hair as he turned his head toward her.
"Just when do you think we can count on growing
up?" he asked.

"No doubt you fancy yourself a wit." Louise let her
lips quirk upward in a disdainful smile. "But should
you really be asking for information, I'd say that
until you leave the safe and boyish confines of the Point,
you will all remain adolescents."

"Well, it's nice to have your fortune told." Dick
laughed then looked down at her. "Be your age,
Louise," he said. "False teeth and rheumatism will
get you soon enough."

"Do you think, because I don't enjoy this," she
made a sweeping gesture of the room, "that I'm almost senile?"

She turned to look at him, her black eyes blazing
with fury, and he answered gravely: "No, I don't.
Maybe you have gone beyond us, having a job and

rubbing elbows with older men and women. But I think it's a pity."

"With a war on? How can you stand there and say you want to be a little boy? When there's fighting to be done, sacrifice, suffering . . ."

"Don't wave a flag." Dick's voice was low but it had lost its lazy drawl. "Mrs. Parrish is in the war—right up to her neck. But she could be your granddaughter."

"All right." Louise spoke coolly again. "Enjoy yourself, my little man," she said sweetly, setting her cup on the mantel, "but don't criticize me because I want a bigger life than you do."

"You don't want a bigger life." Dick was crudely frank. "You've just got the same old grouch. You want more money than Carrol has. You can't afford to enjoy the young and the happy poor because you have to stir around and get it."

"And I will." Louise dropped her mask and Dick saw how cold and determined her face was, how thin her mouth beneath its painted curves. He reached out, laid a hand on her arm and said: "I'm sorry I said that, Louise. You've got a right to the kind of life you want. I hope you get it. You've concentrated long enough."

She brushed away from him, her head high. Groups were scattered about the long room and she looked them over disdainfully before she went on to the library. Penny and Terry were there, feeding dance records to a victrola, and Penny looked up with a welcome.

"Come on in," she urged. "We're going to have some dancing. Terry, you start it off with Louise and the others will follow."

"No thanks." Louise walked to a table, chose a cigarette from a box, and Penny's eyes widened. Leaning against the table and bending toward the lighter Terry held for her, she was a glamorous arc, from her black hair to her gold sandals, and as the flame spurted her gaze swept upward. "Zowie!" Penny said to herself. "Exit, Miss Parrish."

"Everything is running smoothly now," she told David and Carrol, interrupting an intricate tango they were executing in the hall. "I have my victims shut up in the library." She washed her hands together gleefully, the villain in a melodrama, but whirled at a voice behind her.

"This is my dance," Terry said. "Does my pursuit please you?"

"Oh, Terry!" Penny sighed as she fell into step. "Why didn't you stay where I left you?"

"Because, for some reason I can't understand, you wanted to show Louise how devoted I am. I always try to please." He left her dancing alone while he flung out his arms and hunched his shoulders. "Doesn't *this* suit you?"

"Of course it doesn't. Louise thinks you're so wonderful. She looked forward to seeing you . . ."

"Now, I know," he cut her off, "why you want Louise to think you copped me away from the other girls. Would it help if we dance straight through the library?"

"You . . ." Penny tried to pull loose from him but he spun her around and winked at Carrol over her shoulder.

"It's all right, angel," he said into Penny's ear. "Don't get upset. I really don't mind dancing with you."

And Sunday was worse. The game room rang with shouts and the clatter of ping pong balls; luncheon was an elastic meal served when anyone was hungry; but Terry continued to dog Penny's footsteps, and Louise roamed about in a black dress, with an exotic bang hanging over her forehead and the look of a lost French poodle.

When five o'clock came and cars were lined before the door, Penny was glad to speed the departing guests. Terry had agreed, amid the hilarious scramble at the door, to share his club coupe with Louise, but he let her wait while he took both of Penny's hands in an intimate farewell.

"Good-by, my sweet," he said, leaning so close to her that she pulled back and longed to slap the teasing face that grinned at her. "Write to me every day."

"I wish I could murder him. I wish I could tear him limb from limb," she stormed when the door was closed.

"You asked for it." David, waiting for Carrol to drive him back to the Point, told her. "Get your coat and come with us and you'll feel better."

"I'll never feel better until I get even with him." She stamped up the stairs and amused voices coming from Carrol's sitting room did nothing to restore her good humor.

"I'll have the last laugh, yet," she popped her head in to tell her mother and Mr. Houghton. "I'll fix him if it's the last thing I do."

★

CHAPTER X

SORROW AT GLADSTONE

"Aunt Marjorie?" Carrol tapped lightly on the door and Mrs. Parrish sat up in bed.

"Yes, dear, what is it?" she answered, looking at the hands of the traveling clock that pointed at eight. "Come in, dear."

Carrol pushed open the door and trailing her quilted robe, sat down on the side of the bed. "I'm worried about Daddy," she said. "Elfreda told me that he isn't going down to breakfast this morning; that he's had his tray sent up."

"Perhaps he's tired. We had a rather strenuous week end, you know." Mrs. Parrish fumbled with her pillows and Carrol leaned over to wedge them behind her.

"No," she said, rubbing her troubled eyes, "he didn't eat his breakfast. His valet showed me the tray. And he said—oh, Aunt Marjorie, he said he thought Daddy should have the doctor."

"Well then, by all means let's have him." Mrs. Parrish threw back the covers and as Carrol stood up,

135

reached to the foot of the bed for her dressing gown. "I'd rather see him first, though. Suppose we both go in, just as if we're coming to scold him for being so lazy. He may be perfectly all right, you know, and might not like our calling a doctor without consulting him."

"All right, Aunt Marjorie. I'll slip into a dress and meet you."

"Just give me five minutes, and don't worry."

But she, herself, was worried when Masters opened the door for them. Langdon Houghton lay on his side, his eyes dull with fever, his cheeks flushed.

"Good morning," he said with an effort. "Sorry not to come down to breakfast, but I feel lazy."

"Daddy." Carrol ran across the room and dropped down beside the bed. She knew when she laid her hand against his burning cheek that there was no need for pretense. "Shall I call Dr. Cornwall?"

He moistened his parched lips, lifted his hand to stroke her hair, then let it fall again. "Better call him," he whispered, closing his eyes.

Dr. Cornwall came and left. Two nurses came, starched and rustling with competence; and a specialist was rushed from New York. All through the day Carrol sat in the shadows of her father's room or hovered outside the door. When, at last, evening brought him sleep, relief from probing fingers, from medicines and tests, she slipped downstairs.

"Aunt Marjorie," she asked, "he's very ill, isn't he?"

"Yes." Mrs. Parrish standing beneath the portrait of Carrol's mother, sighed. "He's very ill. I've been standing here wondering how to talk to you, looking at your mother for help." She took Carrol's hand, holding it tightly in hers as she led her into the library. "If I were talking to Penny," she said slowly, when they were sitting on a broad bench before a fire that crackled with bright dancing goblins, "I'd try to pretend that nothing is very wrong."

"But Aunt Marjorie. I'd rather face the truth."

"I know you would. And that's why I've decided to tell you exactly what Dr. Cornwall and Dr. Brooks told me. It's very grave, dear—a condition he's had, and that has been growing, steadily, for months."

"I've known it for a long, long time." Carrol sat very straight, her hands clasped in her lap. "Daddy has known it, too. That's why he wanted the party, wanted me to have a good time." She turned, rested both hands on the bench, and leaned close to Mrs. Parrish. "How long will I have him?" she asked tensely.

"Carrol . . ."

"Please, Aunt Marjorie. I can stand the truth and getting used to the thought of losing him better than I could a shock. And I'd rather hear it from you than from a doctor. How long will it be?"

"A few weeks, dear, at the most."

"Thank you, Aunt Marjorie." She stood up and Mrs. Parrish reached for her. Carrol was so unlike Penny. Penny would have thrown herself against her mother, sobbing. But she never could have told the stark truth to Penny as she had to Carrol. What could she add? What could she do for this child who was facing her future so bravely?

"I must go to Daddy, now," Carrol was saying, with only her tightly clenched hands to show her suffering. "I want every minute with him."

There were days when Mr. Houghton was better. Days when he joked with them, when he said, "I think I'll get up tomorrow." And on those days they played games with him, read to him, and brought him small surprises. But bad days followed the good ones. On those days they stood outside his room, waiting for any word of the brave struggle going on behind his closed door. And slowly, inexorably, the good days disappeared.

"Marjorie," he whispered to Mrs. Parrish one morning when the first hint of spring was in the air, "I'd like to talk to David today."

"I'll call, Lang. I'll talk to his Tactical Officer, and I'm sure he'll let David come."

She bent over him and he took her hand between his thin fingers, turning her wedding ring and saying as he looked at it: "I did want one more talk with Dave."

"Oh, I hope you'll have it, Lang. Many of them."

"No." His eyes lifted from the ring to her face. "You know I won't. Dave can't get back in time. And that's why . . ." He paused for breath and went on weakly, "I must entrust so much to David. Poor boy, he's young for so much responsibility."

"But he loves Carrol so deeply, dear. She's David's world."

"I know that. You can't realize what it means to me, Marjorie, to know that I'm leaving Carrol with a mother and father like you and Dave. And with David. Once you wanted to thank me for something . . . and now I . . ."

"And now I still want to thank you for giving us Carrol. Oh, Lang, dear," her tears blinded her but she lifted their clasped hands and laid his against her cheek, "we love you both so much."

He sighed and closed his eyes. "It has been so beautiful," he murmured, "these last four years."

His hand relaxed in hers and her fingers reached quickly for his pulse. It was beating fitfully and she ran to call the nurse.

"Come quickly, David," she said into the phone. "Penny is on the way for you." Then she paced her room until she heard him on the stairs.

"Is he—is he all right?" David asked as she hurried him along the hall.

139

"Yes. But I think he's only waiting for you. Oh, David, if we could just help him."

"And Carrol?"

"She's in there with him, darling."

She opened the door softly, felt the pressure of his hand, then it closed behind him.

David tiptoed across the room. Carrol was on her knees beside the bed, her face on the pillow beside her father's. She held his hand tightly against her breast, and he thought they were both asleep until Carrol's dark-fringed eyes opened. "Here's David, Daddy," she said softly. "Shall I go away for a little while?"

"No, honey. There must never be any secrets between you and David."

"There never will be, Uncle Lang." David knelt beside Carrol and put his arm around her. Then he reached across the covers to touch the thin shoulder, and the three of them were close together.

"I have no fear for Carrol's happiness with you, David." Mr. Houghton spoke slowly, struggling with the words. "It's only the money. There's such a lot of it for you to handle. And so, I've made your father Carrol's legal guardian."

"Yes, Uncle Lang."

"And it's invested . . . government bonds and stocks . . ." He sighed, waited a moment and said, so weakly that David strained to hear, "But even so . . ."

"Don't worry, Uncle Lang, Dad will help us. Just know that Carrol is all that really matters."

Slowly the tired head nodded. "You love her, don't you, David?"

"I love her more than life itself." David looked deep into Carrol's eyes. "I pledge you, Carrol," he said solemnly, "that nothing—not war, or separation, or anything that life may hold, can ever come between us."

"Thank you . . . son . . . That's such a beautiful gift for me to take her mother."

Langdon Houghton's eyes turned to Carrol, rested there for a moment as he smiled at her, then with a tired sigh, they closed, and his hand lay lifelessly in hers.

"Daddy." Carrol pressed her face into the pillow, her lips against her father's cheek. "Don't leave me. Please . . . oh, please."

"There, dearest." David lifted her gently and held her in his arms. "He'll always be with us, Carrol."

"But he won't, David. He's gone. He won't be here to walk in the garden with me, or to ride Scamps Lad. I'll call him and he won't come. He won't say 'honey,' ever again . . . or pull me down on the arm of his chair." She pressed her hands against her mouth, moaning through them; "I thought I could go on living without him, but I can't, Davy. I can't!"

David held her tightly, his own tears falling into her

hair, his own heart a dull, leaden ache. But when he had given her into his mother's loving arms; when he had watched kindly Dr. Cornwall prepare a sedative and had seen her drink it, he stumbled down the stairs to sit with his head in his hands.

"It's over, isn't it, David?" Penny crept in to him, white lipped.

"Yes."

"Is Carrol all right?"

"Mums has her."

"I wanted to see Uncle Lang," Penny sobbed. "I wanted to tell him that I'll go on pretending about the Good Fairy that we made up, and to thank him, and to put my arms around him."

"Don't, Pen." He gripped the arms of the chair. "It wouldn't have done any good. Nothing's going to do any good," he said, pounding the chair with his fists. "We've got to go on living without the best friend we ever had."

Then he flung himself out of the house, wondering how the sun could still be shining.

★

CHAPTER XI

GIFTS OF LOVE

Spring unfolded slowly and timidly. Little leaves stayed wrapped in their warm red blankets, swaying on the end of twigs like small papooses, afraid to trust Mother Nature and a temperamental sun. Grass blades clung to each other. They peeked through brown ambush at shivering robins; then, straight little soldiers on duty, braced themselves for battle against a belligerent wind. Behind the long windows of Gladstone heavy eyes watched for the spring that was so loathe to bring its promise of life.

Carrol went quietly about her duties; Penny pushed her career aside and hurried into town only three afternoons a week so that she and Carrol might spend their mornings on horseback. Bobby came home for the Easter holidays, tall and straight in his cadet uniform; and Tippy clung to him, partly from habit and partly because he was reassuringly male and forceful.

"We gotta do something to make Carrol happier," he said one morning when she had trailed him to a bench beside the tennis court. "It makes me feel awful sad to see her looking so thin."

"It does me, too." Tippy thought about Carrol and tears clouded her eyes. "She just plays cribbage with Mums, and rides Floridian, and sometimes she goes to see David. Carrol doesn't ever cry," she said, using her pink gingham skirt for a handkerchief. "Do you suppose she gets awful lonesome when she's by herself?"

"Sure, she does." Bobby bounced a tennis ball morosely, then gave it a kick. "I wish we had some kind of a present to give her," he muttered.

"But she's rich." Tippy wiped her eyes again and shook her head. "And we're rich now, too. I heard Mummy tell Penny that Uncle Lang fixed it so we'd have an awful lot of money." Then she said from the great wisdom of her seven years: "You can't buy things, Bobby, to make it easier for rich people to bear their troubles."

"No . . . but . . ." He bit his lips in an effort to untangle his thoughts. "I meant a present of love, I guess. Sort of doing something nice and . . ."

"I see." Tippy sat up straight and smoothed her skirt that ruffled out below her navy blue sweater. "We might give her something that belongs to us. Something that we like a lot and that—that's a comfort to us."

Her mind roamed among her treasures and as there

was no hooting contradiction to her proposal, it rested upon her best-beloved and eldest daughter. "Why, Georgia could help anyone through anything," she declared, thinking fondly of the trials she and her child had met and weathered together. "Even when I'm punished or lonesome, or when you aren't nice to me, Georgia can be a comfort to me. I spect she'd be a big help to Carrol, too."

"But she's just a doll, Tip. I didn't mean anything like that." Bobby tried to dash her hopes by making very grand counter-suggestions, but Tippy saw peace for Carrol if Georgia could companion her and was not to be dissuaded.

"She's the very thing," she argued, stubborn and determined in her offer. "I'll go and get her ready and explain to her, and I'm sure she won't mind. Of course, it will nearly kill me to give her up, but lots of mothers have to send their children off on visits."

So that was why Carrol, coming wearily into her room after having driven Penny to the station, saw a very small young lady, hatted, coated, and befurred, sitting in a low chair. Her cardboard suitcase rested on the rug at her feet and she smilingly held out her arms in stiff greeting.

Carrol closed the door and crossed the room to stand before the unblinking guest. "Hello, Georgia," she said. Her throat tightened at the simplicity with which Tippy had shown her love and she dropped to her knees, burying her face against the broadcloth and shiny pearl buttons that covered the hard little body. Tears came; blessed, healing tears. And she sat on the floor, her arms around the doll, until the tears dried on her lashes and Georgia's hand dropped down onto the quiet head that lay sleeping in her lap.

The sun rose high in its sky; the green soldiers became a vast army on the lawn, and the leaves fluttered their blankets earthward, while Georgia kept vigil in the quiet room.

Mrs. Parrish opened the door softly, closed it again, and kissed a big-eyed Tippy. "Go have your lunch now," she whispered. "Quietly, so you won't wake her."

"Do you think she found my knife?" Bobby asked when they were on the stairs.

"I don't believe she has," his mother answered, reaching out to kiss the clipped curls that on the step below were level with her lips. "But she will when she wakes."

"I put it on the window seat with a piece of wood she can whittle on, and I left a note so she'll know it's the knife Uncle Lang gave me; and to be careful because I keep it awful sharp. I hope she sees it."

Carrol found the knife and the note when she wakened from the first healing sleep she had known for days. She had carried Georgia and her suitcase to the window seat, and mindful of the immaculate state in which Tippy always kept her child, was removing Georgia's rumpled coat. When she saw the precise penmanship that was a painstaking tribute to Weyburn Military Academy, she laid Georgia on the cushions, reached for the knife and piece of wood, and sat holding them loosely in her hands. So much love. So much love from a little sister and brother who were giving their dearest treasures to ease her heartache. So much love from Penny, she thought, who gave her days; from Aunt Marjorie, who gave a mother's devotion. So much love from a whole family that was hers. Hers. No one could ever fill the great void her father had left—but she still had a whole family to love. And she had David. She looked out at the trees that shook their heads sadly at her. She had David, but only for a little while, they reminded. The precious hours she might share with him were slipping away. Soon they, too, would be but memories. She could whittle then; she could help Tippy dress and undress Georgia. But now . . . She dropped the knife and bit of stick into the pocket of her dirndl, snatched up Georgia, and ran downstairs.

"Aunt Marjorie," she called from the hall. "Oh, Aunt Marjorie!"

"Yes, darling." Mrs. Parrish came from the dining room, a napkin-covered tray in her hands. "I was just bringing you a combination lunch and afternoon tea."

"Oh, but look!" Carrol held out Georgia and

brought the knife from her pocket. "Lunch doesn't matter, compared with these. With all of you—and David. I still have so much, Aunt Marjorie."

"Dear," Mrs. Parrish set the tray on a table and smiled, "if 'much' means us—you have us, Carrol, always."

"But not David. I've just begun to realize that . . ." She brushed away a tear with Georgia's fuzzy mat of yellow curls and Mrs. Parrish finished her sentence for her.

"That you must steel yourself for another loss," she said quietly. "I know, darling."

"And I don't want to miss any time with him." Her head came up, she tucked Georgia under her arm and held out her hand. "Let's go see him," she begged. "Let's have a jelly date with him in the Boodler's, like the other girls."

"I'd like to." Mrs. Parrish took the thin hand in her soft, warm one and held it tightly. "But David called while you were asleep and asked me to send you over. He very emphatically ordered me to stay away."

"Why, Aunt Marjorie!"

"Isn't he awful?" Mrs. Parrish laughed and lifted the napkin from the tray. "He also ordered you to eat something and, altogether, was very masterful and determined. We'll have to mind him."

Carrol looked down at the tray. "Could I just eat the chicken sandwich?" she asked. "As I ride along?"

GIFTS OF LOVE

"Of course, you can." Mrs. Parrish wrapped the
sandwich in a napkin and watched her add it to the
knife and the doll.

"You're sure you won't go with me?"

"Positive. I wouldn't dare, and besides, I promised
Bobby and Tippy a movie."

They walked together to the garage and she hid a
smile when Carrol settled Georgia in stiff-legged comfort on the seat of her coupe. "I'll tell Tippy her child
has gone for an outing; she'll be pleased."

"David probably won't." Carrol straightened Georgia's hat that obscured her vision and gave her the
knife to hold. Then she turned back to put her arms
around Mrs. Parrish. "And tell the children that . . .
but you know what to tell them, don't you?"

Her grief had left faint shadows, smudges like the
blue of an indelible pencil, and Mrs. Parrish longed
to see them erased. So she nodded briskly, waved her
away, and said: "I'll tell them and they'll be happy.
Now run along, and don't be later than six-thirty or
I'll worry."

"I won't." Carrol backed out her car, swung around
into the drive and waved. She ate her sandwich as she
bowled along the highway, and with a smile that surprised her, held it down to Georgia's shining porcelain
teeth.

How Penny would love this, she thought as she
parked her car and leaned over to give her companion

final instructions. "Don't fall out," she ordered in a motherly tone. And then to be sure that Georgia would remain unmolested, she locked the doors and hurried across the street to Grant Hall.

David met her in the corridor and he swung a paper sack. "About face," he commanded. "We're going places."

"Where?" She took the hand he held out to her and looked up at him with bright interest.

"On a picnic." They crossed the street again and he peered through the car window at the round-moon face smiling against the leather upholstery. "What the dickens have you brought with you?" he asked.

"It's your niece, Georgia." Carrol unlocked the door, gave him the doll to hold while she slid under the wheel, and smiled at his scowl.

"Well, you never can tell what you'll meet these days." He looked about for some place to put Georgia, then got in and set her on his knee. "And why the knife and the woodpile?" he asked, reaching under him. "Have you turned Camp Fire Girl?"

"They're Bobby's donations." Carrol released the brake and added generously: "But I'll let you whittle a bit if you're careful. Now tell me where to go."

"Straight up the road and around a corner and straight again to a parking place."

"You mean . . ." Carrol forgot to start her motor. She pressed the gas throttle, worked the gears, and when nothing happened, turned in a muddle to David. "I'm so confused," she explained. Then she dropped pretense and said softly: "We're going to walk along Flirtation Walk, aren't we?"

"Yes, darling, I thought we would."

"Oh, David." Her eyes held stars as she looked at him. "We said once, that we wouldn't walk there until you were a first classman. And we've waited so long it doesn't seem possible that we're going to do it. What made you decide on today?"

"Because it's spring, and beautiful, and because this seems to be the day for it. It wasn't entered into lightly, Miss Houghton," he informed her. Then he added seriously: "Flirtation Walk has been a goal to you and me. We haven't gone wandering up and down its paths like a lot of couples, joking about the Kissing Rock; because it's been a sort of shrine. We went there when I finished my first year and I told you how much I loved you, and we said we'd come back when I was ready to graduate. Somehow, this is just our day. So let's go."

He reached toward the ignition key, and Georgia, still smiling pleasantly, fell over backwards.

★

CHAPTER XII

FLIRTATION WALK

Carrol and David strolled along a path that was dappled by sunshine through the feathery green of the trees. They talked of David's life at the Point and he related small happenings, bits of news and gossip, just as he had before Carrol's father became so ill. They were happy, absorbed in each other, until David stopped and said with a frown:

"We've passed the fork where you were supposed to decide if we would go by the Kissing Rock or along the river. We'll have to go back."

"No, we won't." Carrol stopped too, but she smiled.

"But it's tradition. The girl has to stop and choose."

"I chose. I didn't stop, but," she looked at him shyly, "I saw the fork and I said to myself, 'now sister, make up your mind which way you're going.' You were talking so fast and I remembered it from the other time, so I just—just . . ." Carrol blushed at her own temerity but she gave his hand a tug and finished her sentence a step ahead of him. "I decided on this path and guided you into it."

GLORY BE!

"Well, isn't that something!" David followed her but he leaned over her shoulder to tease: "Pretty sure of yourself, weren't you?"

"I—I think so." She dropped back beside him and looked up at him tenderly, soberly. "I wish I were as sure of everything as I am of how much. . . ."

"Don't say it yet!" David began to run and Carrol, because her hand was tight in his, kept up a fleet pace beside him. The path rose along the side of a cliff, and beyond several bends in its winding way, it passed beneath an overhanging shelf of stone that was known to cadets of all generations, as the Kissing Rock. Tradition decreed that no girl must pass, unkissed, beneath it; and when they reached its shadow David swung Carrol about until she leaned against its solid back rest, then he faced her squarely. "I've got a present for you," he panted. "I thought I couldn't wait another second but you can finish your sentence first."

"Why, David," Carrol, too, was breathing quickly and she wiped her hot forehead, "how can I remember now what I was going to say then?" she parried.

"Okay. You were going to say you love me—but we'll skip it until I show you something." He jerked off his cap, pulled his pocket handkerchief from it, and laying it on the ground, knelt to sort among its contents.

"David Parrish, you're still the most conceited boy I ever knew!" Carrol pretended indignation but she leaned over to see what he was taking from the handkerchief.

"Sit down here beside me," he invited. "You can't see so far away."

A small box, very new and white, lay with his Boodlers' book, a knife, a fountain pen, and a collection of odds and ends needed in his day. "Pick up the box," he pointed. "Take a look."

So they sat on the ground under the majestic roof and Carrol reached for the box. She pressed the clasp and breathed a long-drawn "O-o-h" as the lid snapped back. A carved gold ring was pinched between white velvet; a small duplicate of David's heavy class ring. It was etched in a design that means so much to every West Pointer, and a large sparkling diamond was embedded in its center.

"A 'miniature!' Oh, David!" She lifted the ring from its box and David's hand closed over hers.

"Wait a minute. There's something I want to ask you before you put it on," he said, his voice tense as her blue eyes came up to meet his. "It's pretty important to us both."

"Yes, David?"

"Will you marry me, Carrol? The day after I graduate?"

155

"Oh!" The color drained from her face, her hands holding the ring trembled, but her voice was steady. "There's the war, David. Because of the war . . ."

"I know. It's because of the war that I want you to. You see," he put his arm around her and pressed her head against his shoulder, keeping it there with his cheek, "when you had Uncle Lang it was different. I didn't have the right to bring extra suffering into your life. Now—now you can't be more unhappy than you are, even when I have to go. And we can be together. At least, for a little while." He moved his lips against her bright hair, said softly: "I love you so much, Carrol."

"And I love you, David." She turned the ring over and over in her fingers. "I know Daddy would be glad," she thought aloud. "He wouldn't want me to grieve and be lonely, would he?" Then without waiting for an answer, she held the ring out to him and smiled into his seriousness. "Put it on, Almost-Lieutenant Parrish," she urged. "Let's be romantic."

David slipped the ring over her slender finger and when it was on they sat admiring their two hands held out before them.

"Twins." Carrol said, wriggling her finger and watching the stone catch the light. "Except that you have a sapphire. How did you ever manage the gorgeous diamond?"

"Gram kicked through. She has one she's going to

give Penny some day and she wanted us to have this one now." David's voice was full of pride as he added: "It's pretty darn good-looking, isn't it?"

"It's beautiful. It's the most beautiful thing I ever had in my life. Oh, Davy," she sighed blissfully, "I'm happy. I didn't realize that, even for a little while, I could be so happy."

"And that's the way I want to keep you." He took her face between his two hands and kissed her tenderly. "There will be lots of times when the hurt will be pretty bad," he said, "but if you can just keep your mind on June the fourth, and know that we're going to have a swell time together, it will be easier. We are going to have a swell time," he repeated.

"I know we are." She leaned against him, careful that her hand in her lap displayed the ring to its best advantage. "Won't it be fun to tell Penny and your mother?"

"They know all about it." David grinned at her surprised upward look. "How do you suppose I got the diamond? And why do you think Mums sent you up here? Sure. Everyone knew of my noble intentions, but you."

"Well, that's a fine way to treat me." Carrol thought it over for a few seconds, then decided amiably: "I'm glad of it. Now I won't have to be embarrassed about explaining. I can just talk quite casually about the wedding plans."

"Are we going to have a wedding?" he groaned. "I mean a big one, with people?"

"We are if you don't mind too much." Carrol was amused by his timidity but she said seriously: "You see, Davy, Daddy and I used to talk about my wedding. We would sit on the terrace, with the stars out and Daddy smoking, while he told me about marrying Mother. We used to talk about what I would wear and how it would be, and it was always in June. Mother was a June bride. And I'd like to do it just the way he wanted—not having so many people of course, only the ones we love and our best friends."

"Then we'll have a wedding," David got up and held out his hands. "Time *fugits*," he said with a matter-of-fact sigh. "If we hurry we can skip a few stones on the river and eat our lunch, then I'll have to hustle back."

"You're always hustling back. You can't even take time to become properly engaged." Carrol grumbled, but she went down to the river with him and helped spread the sandwiches and tepid malted milks on a rock.

"This is the way all our meals will be," David said, "picnics."

"Oh, no they won't." Carrol took a bite of pickle; made a face, either from the acid or his words, and retorted: "I'm going to cook all the fancy things

Trudy taught me. I can make biscuits and cake and I can broil a super-duper steak."

"Whoopee!" David pitched his empty cup into the river as he let out the yell. "I'm getting me a real wife!"

"Well, what did you think you were getting, a hothouse plant?"

"I didn't know. I was afraid that Perkins and a couple of maids might move in with us. I've seen ads about dishpan hands."

"And I've seen ads for soap flakes and rubber gloves. And what's the difference anyway? We're going to have fun—but of course we'll take off our rings."

"Our rings? Our rings?" David exploded when he caught the meaning in her words. "Where do you get this 'our ring' stuff?"

"Why, Davy, you know you'll want to help me wash the dishes. We'll tie an apron over your pretty uniform and . . . Oh, darling," she tossed the crust of her sandwich after his floating cup and stretched up her arms, "I am happy."

"That's all I ask." He saw tears on her lashes and said quickly, teasingly: "It's worth giving up my bachelor freedom—it's even worth having to wear an apron."

"Then I'll clean up this mess; alone, believe it or

not, if you will carve a few hacks into a stick Bobby
gave me." She took the knife and bit of wood from
her pocket and went on to explain: "I want him to
know how much I appreciate it; so you carve, I'll
watch you, and together we'll make our plans."

Reaching over, she stuffed the papers and her cup
into the sack and whisked through her housekeeping
by tossing the sack into the river. Then she leaned
toward David, watching his knife cut clean, sure
strokes.

His cap was on the back of his head, he sat cross
legged, and now and then he looked up to smile at her
Little slivers of wood fell between them and when the
unmistakable head of a horse became outlined David
glanced at his watch and snapped the knife shut
"Time to go," he said reluctantly.

Georgia was waiting placidly in the car and after
Carrol had left David and was on the highway, she
smiled down at her. She felt foolish when she flashed
her ring for Georgia to see, but the urge to talk to
someone was too strong to resist so she told Georgia
all about it. "And you see," she concluded, "we'll just
walk in, very nonchalantly, and we'll be cool, calm
and collected."

But she reckoned without the Parrish family. Al
though reduced in number, the Parrish enthusiasm
was unchanged, and four eager faces were watching
from the drawing room windows. Carrol braked her

car, ran up the shallow steps; and when she opened the door, was wrapped in an entanglement of arms that would have made an octopus feel weak and futile.

"By gum, he actually got her," Penny beamed, clinging to Carrol's hand on which the new ring blazed. "I knew she couldn't resist him."

"I didn't even try." Carrol laughed and kissed them, one at a time, before she bent down to restore Georgia to her rightful mother. "Thank you, Tippy, darling," she said softly. "We've had a wonderful day together."

"Was Georgia there when you got engaged to David?" Tippy's small face lifted to ask.

"Well, not exactly. She . . ." Before Carrol could explain that the interlude might have been dull for Georgia, Penny pulled at her.

"Who cares what Georgia did?" Penny cried. "We want to know about you and David, so let's group ourselves some place." Then she saw the quiet disappointment in Tippy's face and she hugged her and whispered: "Of course, we know it was all Georgia's doing. She really fixed it."

"Do you think so, Penny?" Tippy looked with admiration on her child and trailed behind to slip her hand in Bobby's. "The knife helped too," she assured him. "Carrol will tell us so."

And as if answering her, Carrol chose that moment to pull out the knife and the half-carved horse's head. "David started this," she told Bobby, coming back to

161

put her arm around him. "He didn't have time to finish it, but perhaps we can work on it before you go back to school. Thanks, loads, Bobby; David and I loved sitting by the river and whittling."

His face lighted up but Penny let out a howl. "Whittling!" she shrieked; from the corner of the sofa where, anticipating dramatic disclosures, she had ensconced herself. "Don't tell me you didn't plan about getting married!"

"We did both." Carrol laughed and dropped down beside her. "Oh, Aunt Marjorie," she cried to Mrs. Parrish who sat across the room, amused and patiently waiting, "You have the *nicest* son!"

"I thank you." Marjorie Parrish bobbed her head, then jumped up to curl into a corner on the other end of the sofa. "Everyone knows how much I love my daughter, so tell us what you planned."

"Well," Carrol put her hands in the pockets of her skirt and studied the tips of her white Oxfords as she tapped their soles together. Her face became grave and she moistened her lips. "David wants the wedding just as I want it," she said slowly, "and I feel that I must have everything the way Daddy and I had planned."

"Of course, darling." Mrs. Parrish nodded, then frowned at Penny who was eager to interrupt. "How was that?"

"Right here at home. With a real bride's dress and

everything." She looked up from the contemplation of her shoes to ask uneasily: "Do you think people would criticize it, Aunt Marjorie?"

"Certainly, they won't." Penny could wait no longer. "I think it's a perfectly lovely idea. And I'll be your maid of honor."

"Would you like to, Pen?"

"Don't be silly." Penny wriggled with excitement. "I've planned on it for years."

"And can we be in it, too?" Tippy leaned against Carrol's knee and raised her face eagerly. "Bobby would look awful nice in his uniform."

"We'll let you know later." Penny scowled and dislodged her, but she looked to Bobby for assistance. "This is no place for men," she flattered, "so take your satellite and depart." She watched them go before she breathed a sigh of pleasure and interrupted again. "Start over," she demanded. "I missed something."

"Why, I was only saying that I want it to be just as if Daddy were here. I want you all close to me." She leaned over to straighten a cigarette box on the coffee table and asked without looking up: "Aunt Marjorie, when will Uncle Dave be home?"

"He hopes to be here in time for David's graduation, about the first of June he thought. Why, darling?"

"Because," she leaned back among the pillows again

and her throat was tight when she tried to answer. "I want him to give me away."

Mrs. Parrish reached for her hand, held it tightly, and Carrol went on: "If he can't come—I want it to be you. You wouldn't feel hurt would you, Aunt Marjorie, because I asked Uncle Dave first?" She turned her head and Mrs. Parrish pulled her gently to her shoulder.

"I'd feel hurt if you didn't," she smiled, "because I know that nothing would make him happier."

"And even if he is here," Carrol said softly, "I want you to stand right beside us, too. You and Penny and Bobby and Tippy. The whole family—and Trudy. I want Trudy with us."

"She'll love it." Penny tried to ease the tension by exclaiming: "Now she'll know why she's been saving her good black dress."

"She's going to have a new one. A soft blue one she ordered from a fashion catalogue." Carrol's eyes grew tender thinking of the amount of money her father had set aside for Trudy. She got up and walked to the mantel, stood looking down into the empty grate. "There's just one more thing," she tried to say above the labored beating of her heart, not daring to look at them. "I want to come down the stairs, all the way to David . . . alone . . . just with Daddy. We planned . . ." Her head went down on the cold marble, David's ring crushed against her lips. "I can't talk about it any more, Aunt Marjorie," she sobbed into the arms that held her. "It's beginning to hurt again."

"Of course, you can't." Penny dashed a quick hand across her own eyes and leaped into action. "It's almost dinner time but I'll challenge you to a quick game of ping pong," she cried. "Why, we have a whole month to get ready for the wedding!"

★

CHAPTER XIII

A Feud with Flowers

"It's a fine thing," David said to Penny, coming into the house and watching Perkins whisk away his bag, "I come home for my last week end before graduation, and do I find my bride? I do not," he answered himself.

"Well, pet, that's because she's gone shopping for you." Penny gave him a pat to placate him. "She and Mums went in to look at dresses."

"Dresses! Ye gods!" David was far from mollified. "She has dozens of dresses. And what are those for?" he asked, pointing to a pile of sheets Penny held over her arm. "Don't tell me she's wasting my precious time buying more linen!"

"These are for me, my fine friend," Penny said with dignity. "I suppose, in your frenzy over your wedding trip—all the way to Fort Knox, Kentucky—you've completely forgotten that I'm going away, too."

"Well, bless me, if I hadn't." David's grin was wide. "I guess I thought you'd be going along with us." He sat down astride a chair and admired her over

167

its back. "It's going to seem pretty awful not having you hanging around," he said. "Why don't you come down and visit us?"

"Idiot." Penny flopped the sheets over her shoulder and marched toward the stairs. "Don't forget my Career with a capital C," she flung back. "I'm starting it right after you and Carrol drive off through the rice and old shoes."

"It's a lucky thing my future wife has a car with five good tires," David answered, dismissing her career for his own good fortune. "Now that I can't have one for a graduation present." Then he followed to stand at the foot of the stairs. "Heard anything from Dad, yet?"

Penny laid her sheets on a step and sat down beside them. "Not a word," she answered. "That might mean he's on his way or it might mean he can't make it. What do you think?"

"I wouldn't know. But I hate to graduate without him. Well, he still has two weeks." David leaned against the newel post and looked up at her. "So you're really going to do it," he said.

"I really am." Penny nodded emphatically and he asked:

"What about the great Hayes?"

"Terry?" she shrugged and pulled the sheets onto her lap, preparatory to flight. "He still calls up, if that's what you want to know."

"Hasn't he gone in for a black-haired gal instead of a brown?"

"No. No, he hasn't." Penny's voice was disgusted. "I fixed it all up. I simply *flung* them together. And what does he do? *Nothing.* He's a great disappointment to me."

"Carrol said that would happen. She said you were too obvious about it. You should have acted jealous."

"Obvious . . . jealous?" she threw her hands wide. "I simply *shrieked* with jealousy. I pleaded with him to give her up, to keep away from her!"

"Why didn't it work?"

"He hadn't seen her." Penny grabbed her sheets and scuttled up the stairs but David laughed and followed her.

He sat beside the desk and with his hands clasped behind his head watched her ink her name on the sheets. "Do you have to furnish all that stuff?" he asked, when she yelped over a blot.

"Yep. The letter from the manager said 'bedding' but you know how Mums is. You'd think I was going to Alaska. And talk about Carrol having a trousseau— you ought to see mine. I've got more dresses than I ever had in my life. Would you like me to model for you?" She looked up eagerly but he shook his head.

"Not today, thanks. I wish Carrol would come home." He got up to wander restlessly about the room and Penny became absorbed in her inking. As she finished a sheet she laid it on the bed and when the telephone rang, rolled across the white expanse to answer it.

"Hi," she said blithely, but wrinkling up her nose at David. "We were just talking about you." She listened for a moment then groaned in pretended anguish. "Oh, Terry, I'd love to but I can't. No, really I can't. You see . . . You see . . ." She opened her mouth every few seconds, feeling like a gold fish gasping at the top of its bowl, but the voice on the other end of the line paid no attention to her. "Now, wait a minute, Terry," she protested finally, in one good gulp. "I'd love to go to the officers' hop at Dix but I can't. We're having a wedding out here. No, of course it isn't to be next Saturday night. But you see . . ." Despairingly she held the receiver a foot from her ear and waited. "Why don't you take Louise?" she finally shouted into the jumble of words. The yell that answered her jerked the phone from her tired arm and she leaned over the bed to retrieve it.

"Ask him if he'll ush for the wedding," David said.

She nodded, flinched when she replaced the instrument to her ear, and shouted as soon as she could: "Now, wait a minute. I'll talk about that later but David is in a hurry. He wants to know if you'll be an usher at his wedding. The fourth of June. You will? Swell," she nodded across the room then led the conversation into more pleasant paths. "Dick will ush too and Michael will be best man, and Faith and Denise are bridesmaiding . . . No, Terry, Louise is *not* going to be in the wedding." Then she shook her head helplessly. "Here we go again," she whispered. "What shall I *do?*"

David laughed and came to take the phone. "Hi, Terry," he said. "What's the beef?"

The young man on the other end of the connection, sitting in his bare cubicle that held the scent of new lumber hastily thrown into temporary officers' quarters, ran his hand through already ruffled hair. "Your sister has got me into a mess," he growled, "just a dandy mess."

"How come?"

"By throwing me in the lion's den, to the wolves, to Louise. Listen." He hunched over his slab of a desk that hung from the wall on chains, and began a lengthy and more coherent explanation. "I didn't mind taking Louise home from your delightful little house party," he said. "She told me, confidentially, that she is engaged to a guy, a very rich guy—and I've since found out myself, a very jealous guy."

"Does Penny know that?"

"She would if she'd listen to what I've been trying to tell her. Gosh." Terry lowered his voice and looked toward the flimsy door. "We were having tea one afternoon in Nichole's, Louise and I, and in walks the fiance. Of course, Penny *had* been there, having engineered the rendezvous and producing Louise as the unexpected, but she had done a very neat disappearing act. So there Louise and I sat, twosing, when in comes the guy. He was apoplectic."

"Well," David tried to sound cheery, "that's Louise's worry, not yours."

"No?" Terry sighed and let the desk strain under his elbows. "The guy happens to be my commanding officer. And he doesn't like me now."

"Oh, gosh." David shot a glare at Penny and she snickered. "Couldn't you explain to him that it was an accident?" he asked into the phone.

"I did," Terry answered wearily. "And everything seemed to be all right, on my end, that is, but Louise called that it wasn't on hers and asked me to meet her at the club."

"Oh-oh!"

"And she was crying on my shoulder . . ."

"When the guy walked in again."

"How'd you guess it? The Major, you should say. He's a rich polo-playing Reserve Officer and I'm only a low-ranking Regular. He's awful mad."

David could imagine the little scene into which the Major entered and was glad that Terry was too far away to see his smile.

"It seems," Terry was going on, "that he's been misinformed into believing that I'm a wow with the girls and there wasn't much I could say. He had his mind made up. And he has it made up about my efficiency report, too. Good Lord, Dave," he groaned, "there's a war on. I can't afford to let a thing like this hold me back. It's no time to be silly."

"You're right about that." David's voice was sure when he asked: "What do you want Penny to do? She'll do it." He listened for some seconds, said: "Okay, fellow, I'll ring you around eight," and hung up the receiver.

Penny sat on the chaise longue and watched him come back to her. "I didn't mean for it to happen," she said before he could scold, "but I'm even with him now."

"Aren't you ashamed of yourself?"

"Well," she looked up at him and stopped a giggle. "I'm sorry he got into trouble, but it serves him right for butting into my affairs."

"That's childish," David answered sternly. "You and Terry keep playing a game of you-slap-me-and-I'll-slap-you-back. After awhile the stings are going to hurt. And, after all, you're interfering with Terry's job."

"No more than he interfered with mine." Penny shook her head stubbornly. "Louise should have told me she had asked the dumb-dodo to meet her at Nichole's, and Terry knew she was engaged to his boss. I'm not going to pretend to some old man that I'm the only girl in Terry's life. You know Mums won't let me go down to Dix, all alone, to a dance. Why," she sat up, stiff and straight and belligerent, "it's absurd to even think of it."

"Then she can go with you. You can both make a fuss over Terry; sort of a family affair." Then he remembered that his father might be home by then, and substituted, "Or Trudy can drive down with you. That way, you could leave early and come home that night."

"Oh law, sugah," Penny drawled, "I sho' would love to go on dancin' with yo' all han'some gen'men fo' the rest of the night—but little Scarlet has to go back to huh colo'ed mammy now." She flipped an imaginary ruffle and hid her face coyly behind her hand. "Mammy's awaitin' out in the big black dark fo' huh sugah-pie."

"You idiot." David had to laugh through his crossness. "Just the same, you're going down there." He strode around the room, stopping before a picture of Carrol and her father on horseback. "One would think," he said absently, "that out of four million soldiers, Louise could get herself engaged to someone beside Terry's boss."

"But that wouldn't be Louise." Penny sank back among the pillows and sighed. "There probably aren't very many unattached rich ones floating around and she couldn't make trouble for us if she found a guy in Oklahoma. I suppose I'll help Terry out, but . . ." A sudden sparkle leaped into her eyes. She snapped her fingers and landed in a jump before the dressing-table and her purse. "Scuse me," she said, elbowing David out of the way so she could spill its contents on the bed. Then she curled herself above it, counting loose change and a carefully folded bill.

"What goes on?" he asked, watching her ruffle through the pages of the telephone directory. But she only grinned and reached for the phone.

She called a number, and while she waited, swayed her shoulders in rhythm to a jaunty whistle. "Hello," she broke off to say. "I'd like to telegraph some flowers. To Fort Dix. To Captain Terry Hayes. One orchid. Umhum, that's right, and you can charge it to Miss Houghton." Then she added in an aside to David, "Don't get nervous, I'll pay Carrol." She listened a moment, nodded, and said again, sweetly, "And I want to enclose a card. Will you take it, please? Just write: Many Happy Returns, and sign it: Penny."

The receiver slammed and she swung off the bed. "That will give him a rough idea of how *I* felt," she said gleefully. "But I do wish I could see his face when he gets it."

"A fool and his money," David retorted, "are mighty soon parted."

He heard the front door close and left her for a whirlwind descent of the stairs. His mother and Carrol

looked up to wave and their hands were still in mid-
air when he had them in his arms. "Gosh, I thought
you were never coming home," he cried, bestowing
kisses impartially.

"It was my fault," Carrol told him. "I lost my
purse; and while that didn't matter so much, I had the
gas ration book in it. Parker kept going around and
around the block, using up more gas, while Aunt Marjorie and I ran in and out of shops. But I found it."
She held the purse triumphantly aloft and David
snatched it from her and tossed it on a chair.

"What did you buy?" he asked.

"Simply divine things," his mother answered.
"Carrol, tell him all about them while I see to my family." She pushed David away and asked: "Is Tippy
all right?"

"Fine."

"And Penny?"

"She's in another mess." David pointed upward.
"You'll have to help her out of it so see if you can
talk some sense into her."

"Oh, dear." His mother picked up her small packages and David led Carrol toward the library.

"It isn't hopeless," he said over his shoulder, "so
don't get too upset."

"I don't know what to do about you, this summer,
Penny." Mrs. Parrish lamented on Sunday afternoon,
sitting by the tennis court and watching Carrol smash

back a hard serve of David's. "Even though Miss Turner is going to stay at the Inn in the village . . ."

"Why, don't you come right out and call a spade a spade, darling," Penny interrupted with a grin. "Miss Turner is going to chaperon me. She'll be on the job this summer and she'll be in the penthouse next winter, and if I do get a part in a play, she'll be the face behind the face behind the footlights. I don't see how anything could happen to me."

"And she's so sweet and happy to be doing it. I have to go with Daddy wherever he'll be sent, but I feel that I ought to leave Trudy for you, too."

"Oh, Mums, I'll be all right." Penny leaned forward and said so low it was almost a whisper: "I'm afraid to even think it, but I do believe Miss Ware has planned to give me a small part in her new play—if I make good this summer, of course."

"I know. She hinted that the day I had lunch with her." Mrs. Parrish stifled another sigh to clap encouragement across the court to Carrol, who had won her point. "I suppose it's selfish," she went on, "but I wish you could be satisfied at home as Carrol was. I would even be glad if you were interested in some nice boy."

"There isn't any nice boy," Penny retorted. "Unless you want to count the long-legged officer who is now bounding across our lawn—and I wouldn't call him 'nice.'" She watched the approaching figure and added: "He looks like he's breathing fire." Then she noted the florist box he swung, and threw up her hands to catch it before it struck her in the face.

"You very smart and comic little beast," Terry said, planting his feet wide apart and glowering at her. "With five officers standing in front of Headquarters . . . hello Mrs. Parrish . . . up rides a boy on a bicycle with a florist box. Orchids! Orchids to an officer in the United States Army! An officer who, by the sweat of his brow, by apologizing and kowtowing for something you started, had just been given a battalion to command. Do you know what that means? It means promotion—a majority! And just when everyone is congratulating me—along you come with a floral tribute."

He stopped for breath and Penny's surprised face cracked in a grin. "It isn't funny!" he shouted, and at that she doubled up with laughter.

"I'm very, very sorry," she managed in her prettiest voice, before she went off into a second gale. She peeked up at his fury; wondered if he were really angry, or if he enjoyed the joke as much as she did. It was hard to tell about Terry. Then she saw Carrol and David leaving the court and lost control again.

"Penny," her mother admonished, "stop being so silly. You should be ashamed to have embarrassed Terry."

"I am." She lifted her head, swallowed a laugh, and dared another look upward. Terry was still standing like a statue of Napoleon and she had difficulty controlling her mouth and scrambling to her feet.

"Sir," she said, clicking her heels, "I surrender my sword to you."

"Hm," he answered, "I don't trust you."

"Would you like me to throw myself at your feet before the assembled audience? Would you like me to bow my head in shame or sign a written confession with a pen dipped in my life's blood?"

"I'd like you to try—only *try* to behave yourself."

"Oh sir, I will. I promise that I will." Penny crossed her heart solemnly and Terry permitted himself a few more glares.

The florist box had bounced from her lap, disgorging its orchid that lay between them, blooming like an exotic flower in the grass, and he bent to pick it up. "Here," he said. "To the victor belong the spoils."

Penny reached out her hand, went a step nearer to look into his eyes. There was a twinkle there. "Shake?" she asked.

"Shake."

Their hands met awkwardly over the transference of the flower and they both grinned.

"I don't understand it," Mrs. Parrish said, "but you two seem to."

"It's very simple." David sat on the arm of her chair and gave Terry a whack with his racket. "They're declaring a temporary truce."

"And he's paying me off with my own flowers." Penny fastened the orchid through the buttonhole of her green sweater. "It doesn't seem much booty," she added, "after a good battle, so I'm collecting some more from a hot dog stand."

She started across the lawn and before he followed her, Terry turned to say: "Mrs. Parrish, she is what is known as a 'holy terror.'"

They were halfway to the drive before Carrol and David could pitch their rackets into bewildered Mrs. Parrish's lap.

"Hey," David shouted. "We're hungry, too. Wait for us!"

★

CHAPTER XIV

FAREWELL WEST POINT

"Well," Penny said, fastening the strap of a sandal, "here we are in June Week." Then she looked up to add: "I think it's pretty swell of you, Carrol, to go through the whole thing as you're doing."

"I want it all perfect for David's sake." Carrol took a wide-brimmed hat from its box and smoothed the transparent pink brim. "He can only graduate from the Academy once; and later, when the boys get together and talk about the hops and the Commandant's garden party, I don't want him to have to say 'we didn't go because that was the year Carrol lost her father.' I want everything to be just right, clear up to our wedding."

"It will be. And you'll be the most beautiful girl at the General's party." Penny looked up at Carrol, glowing and lovely in her trailing pink organza; and unmindful of the damage to the hat or her own lavender net, jumped up to hug her.

"David's the luckiest guy in the world," she said, going to the bed for her floppy leghorn that was tied with American-beauty velvet ribbons reaching to the floor.

"If only your father would come. Why, Penny," Carrol spread her skirts carefully over a chair and sat down. "David graduates tomorrow. We're to be married the day after tomorrow—and not a word. I'm worried."

"Well, you can bet Dad's trying. I feel that he's out there, somewhere, on his way. He was due back four days ago and I know that if he can't make it he'll send a cable. But I do wish he could have seen David win a cup in the horse show."

"And then, there are all the people staying at the hotel; old friends and classmates of his. Aunt Marjorie goes around with them but you know it makes her feel badly to see the Draytons and the Fords watching Michael and Dick. Which reminds me." Carrol turned to look at Penny who was suddenly very busy with a bang she was combing under her hat's drooping brim. "Who was the redhead with Mike yesterday?"

"Sally Fletcher. Cute, isn't she?" Penny gave the bang a swirl and started over. "She visits Mary Jane McGuire a lot."

"Is Mike interested?"

"I think so." Penny had the bang adjusted to her liking and she tilted her head back to look at it. "He's taken her to the hops when I've been with Terry. I offered to let him drag her today but he said he'd made the date with me. Poor Mike, he's so loyal that he's afraid to admit his waning affection even to himself."

"You're a funny generous little thing." Carrol laughed and Penny turned to stare at her.

"Why? If I don't want the gents there's no reason why I should tie 'em to my wrist like a bunch of balloons. Release them, I say. Let them soar off into the blue. They might land in greener pastures." Pleased with her simile, she nodded brightly. "Not bad," she commented. "I must use that when I write my memoirs. Let's see if Faith and Denise are ready."

"You go on," Carrol said. "I have to see Aunt Marjorie. I just remembered a dear friend of Daddy's, a senator, whom I want to ask to the wedding. That's the beauty of inviting people informally," she added as they went along the hall. "It's never too late to telephone."

Faith and Denise were waiting; Faith in pale yellow, and Denise in blue sharkskin. "Beautiful colors," Mrs. Parrish said, adding her fragile green lace to them. "Carrol, these would have been lovely for a rainbow wedding."

"Everyone keeps asking me what colors we're going to have," Penny said on her way down the stairs. "And I'm really proud that I haven't told." She looked at her mother beside her and her arm reached out. "You look younger than any of us," she exclaimed impulsively. "I wish Dad would pop in this afternoon. He'd think he had acquired another daughter while he was gone."

"Thank you, sweet. I wish he would too, not because of my synthetic youth that is due to my fine clothes, but because I don't see how we will get through the next two days without him."

They watched for him all during the garden party, drove quickly to the hotel that David might telephone Gladstone, but there was no news.

"We'll have our dinner," Mrs. Parrish decided, "then we'll go on to the hop. I feel that I should go home early, so if you girls don't mind, I'll take the car and send Parker back for you. David, darling, do one more errand. See if our table is ready."

He started across the lobby that swarmed with girls, and parents, and cadets in their summer uniform of white trousers and formal dress coats, then dodged his way back again to Carrol. "Can't go without my bride," he grinned, taking her away from Dick and Creighton. "Might lose her."

He held her hand in his and bent down to peer beneath the hat's broad brim. "All right?" he asked.

"Happy, Davy."

"Good sport."

They inspected the table that was laid for fourteen and he shook his head because one chair would be empty. "Good thing we aren't superstitious," he said. "If Dad doesn't show up we'll be thirteen."

When they returned to the lobby, the Draytons and the Fords had arrived and both of the officers were in white uniforms. "Uncle Dave would look much handsomer than either Colonel Drayton or Colonel Ford," Carrol whispered before they joined them.

"Wait until you see me," David teased. "My wedding suit, that's my traveling outfit, and future work uniform too, is hanging in my locker shined to the last brass ornament. How's yours?"

"Well, I have several; but they're ready. You haven't lost the ring, have you?"

"Mike says it's safe."

They joined the guests, and all through dinner and the hop were conscious of a sadness. This was the last time they would dance in the softly colored lights; would stand on the balcony of Cullem Hall; would walk through its halls hung with portraits of famous men. Never again, no matter how often they returned, could it be the same. There would be no signs marked "off limits." They would sit in the Officers' Club with the adults. They would talk of the world beyond the gates and not of writs and passes and *femmes*. Something very good was over, and David, standing in the starry June night that seemed so peaceful, squared his shoulders and said to Michael, beside him: "I hope we can take what's coming, Mike."

"We can." Michael gave his head a confident shake and went indoors.

There was no news from Colonel Parrish when the girls hurried home from the hop; no news when they left for the graduation exercises the next morning.

"David will be simply crushed." Penny said, following her mother into the great Field House.

It was filling rapidly and Mrs. Parrish only nodded as she hurried Tippy and Bobby into seats. She stepped back for Faith and Denise, motioned to Carrol, then slipped in beside her, leaving Penny on the aisle.

"You watch David," Penny said. "I'll watch the door."

The corps marched in. The graduating class filed into the front rows of the center section, and Penny leaned toward her mother again. "I hope the speeches will go on and on," she whispered. "It takes a good while to hand out four hundred and fifty diplomas; so perhaps . . ." She straightened up. There was the rustle of people rising from their chairs as the first stirring notes of the *Star-Spangled Banner* filled the air.

Penny listened with her head high. There was no thought of watching the entrance beyond the thousands who blocked her view, as she looked proudly at the banners beside the stage. They were all one flag; from the smallest on its standard to the great rectangle that hung above the rostrum. Eighteen hundred cadets were standing quietly; waiting to fight for it, to die for it if need be. "O'er the land of the free . . . the home of the brave." She sat down soberly. The Commandant began to speak, and the only movement was that of guards walking watchfully about as all eyes but Penny's turned toward the rostrum.

"He'll come, he'll come," she kept saying to herself, long after the Secretary of War had begun his address to the class. And when the Chaplain rose for a prayer, she added her silent plea to his.

The first cadet walked up the steps of the platform to receive his diploma and the building rang with applause. Another followed, and another; and the first quarter of the class had become young officers when Penny left her seat and hurried up the aisle. She edged behind the corps, past temporary bleachers, to the door. "We're over on the other side, Daddy," she whispered. "I'll show you."

Bobby, watching for David to walk up the aisle, turned his head at Denise's nudge; then with a wide grin prodded Tippy to her feet. He slid behind her and pulled her to his lap while the Parrish line moved over. Colonel Parrish, bronzed and lean, smiled down at his wife as he stepped across her knees to the seat between her and Carrol.

"Don't tell me I've missed David," he said, taking both their hands in his. "Not after what I've gone through to get here."

187

"You haven't. There!" Marjorie Parrish jerked her hand away to join the thunderous applause that was largely the corps' response to David's popularity as a cadet. "Oh, you made it, Dave; you made it," she said, blinking back the tears of pride so she could see David shaking hands with the Commandant.

"I had to." Colonel Parrish's hands stung from his message to David; but Michael was on the platform, with three-hundred cadets behind him, and he clapped and grinned with all the ardor of the lowest-ranking plebe. Once he stopped to flick a salute to the military Bobby, and once to pull Tippy between his knees.

"Lord, I was worried," he told them, when they were outside and he and David had expressed their greetings and congratulations in the hearty way peculiar to men. "We had delay after delay in England. Our plane finally landed last night at . . ." He stopped and grinned, "It landed last night," he repeated. "And another one was to pick us right up and bring us to New York. We waited and waited but nothing happened."

"Couldn't you have wired us, Dave?"

"Not from there. We took off before dawn this morning and I could have when we stopped to refuel but I thought I could make it and I didn't want you watching and wondering."

"Well, you got here." Penny was satisfied. "And you're in time for the wedding."

Colonel Parrish looked at Carrol. "Marjorie tells me you're a pretty brave girl," he said, holding her shoulders between his hands and kissing her. "You know how I feel about you, don't you?"

"She knows how we all feel about her." Penny was impatiently excited. "I want to go home and hear all about your trip and show you the wedding presents. Can you go, David?"

"Sure. I'm through here now; as soon as I change."

They parked the cars and sat on benches beside the parade ground while David went through the sally-port and across the stone quadrangle to his barracks. He walked up the familiar stairs and pushed open the door of his room for the last time. For four years it had been his home. He had brought his plebe heart-aches into it; had found comfort and happiness in its bare, Spartan simplicity. Michael was there; half cadet, half officer, as he admired the gold second lieutenant's bars on the blouse he wore above white cadet slacks.

"Thought they might be on crooked," he explained, angling for a better view in his locker mirror.

"They look okay." David sat down on the edge of his scarred study table and laid his cap beside him. "I hate to take off this rig," he sighed, rubbing his chin and looking at his open wardrobe trunk. "Heck, Mike, I wish we could do it all over." He lighted a cigarette and flipped the match at the waste basket. It fell on the floor and he let it lie there. "No more demerits," he grinned. "No more dusting, no more making up my bed before I can sleep."

Michael left his locker and draped an arm across David's shoulder. "See this?" he asked, taking a small jeweler's box from the patch pocket on his blouse. "What makes you think you aren't going to be neat and keep house?"

"Lord." David pushed the box away and unfastened the stiff collar of his blouse. "Here I sit mooning about the past when my girl's waiting for me downstairs." Then he lapsed into study again. "But it has been swell, Mike. You've been a whale of a good room-mate." He got up from the desk and their hands met.

"You'll always be tops with me, Dave," Michael answered. "Happy landings."

"Air Corps stuff." David went to his locker, took off his blouse and tossed it on the springs of an iron cot. "Why the dickens, couldn't you have chosen the Armored Force?"

"Not exciting enough. How could I wish you luck in stuffy Armored Force lingo?"

"I wouldn't know. Happy bumps and plenty of 'em, I guess." He took a pair of polished boots from the locker, tossed a pair of whipcord breeches on top of his blouse, and stood with the boots in his hand.

"Pretty snappy, huh?"

"They'll look darling after a bout with a tank."

They began to dress and when David was tugging

at a boot Michael said: "Some day I'll be flying along a battle front, just cruising slowly at a hundred miles an hour, and I'll see your head sticking out of a tank turret. There goes poor old Dave, I'll say—crawling along like a turtle."

"But crawling." David nodded his head sagely. "You keep 'em flying, boy, and I'll crawl in and out of holes till I get to Berlin. The Army's really going to function now that it's got us."

They inspected each other thoroughly, to be sure no error revealed their recently commissioned status, then David banged the door behind him in the old familiar manner. "See you tomorrow," he called, taking the stairs as he always did, two at a time.

"Oh, David!" a chorus of feminine voices greeted him when he crossed the roadway. And Penny's topped them by shouting: "You look *wonderful!*"

"And twice as broad-shouldered as you did in those skimpy cadet blouses!" his mother cried before he could hush them.

"My gosh, everybody's looking at us!"

"Don't embarrass the boy." Colonel Parrish answered a salute from a passing soldier and watched David from the corner of his eye. David's hand hesitated, then went quickly to his cap. "There's your first salute, son," he said. "How'd you like it?"

"Swell."

"I want to go home," Tippy complained, clinging

191

to her father's hand. "I want to see what you brought me. I'm tired of looking at David."

"Well, believe me, Tip, I'm tired of it, too." David was glad for a place in Carrol's car and he returned the salute at the gate easily now. "Hey," he said when they were going through Highland Falls. "Stop the car and move over, girl. I can drive now."

Carrol laughed and gave him the wheel and he looked down at her. She looked so slender and so small beside him. Somehow, he did feel bigger; and older. More grown up and competent.

"A little later than this, tomorrow," he said, bending his head so that Penny in the back seat couldn't hear: "I'll be saying, 'Wife, reach in the package compartment and find my sun glasses!' "

CHAPTER XV

When Dreams Come True

"Dad, did you ever see such gorgeous wedding gifts?" Penny hovered over the tables in Carrol's upstairs sitting room, pointing out the different pieces of silver.

"It looks as if they have everything."

"Everything but a place to put it. Goodness knows, where they'll find a place to live near Knox. But Carrol doesn't seem to mind." Penny turned her head at shouts from below. "That would be Terry arriving," she informed her father. "He said he could get a twelve hour pass but I didn't believe him."

"Aren't you going down?" Colonel Parrish looked quizzically at her but she answered casually:

"After a while. Someone will put him to work."

Colonel Parrish wondered what was going on in her mind. She had told him about her plans but there was a blank in his understanding of her like a sunspot in a developed film. It might, he reflected, be due to his four months' absence, or it might be a new reticence in Penny, a secrecy that comes with maturity. Bobby had grown, Tippy had lost more teeth, and David was being married, all during his time away from them; so it stood to reason that Penny would change. But he wanted to find no change in her: He wanted her to be exactly as she had been; gay and childishly lavish in the display of her emotions. He searched for words that might bring her closer to him, but she slipped her arm through his and said with the frankness he had feared was gone:

"Terry's a darling, really. I'd hate it like the dickens if anything happened to him."

"Like him a lot?" He tried to sound casual as he lifted a silver dish to examine it.

"Umhum. But he doesn't know it." Then she leaned against the table and looked at him. "Dad," she said, "you have to be awfully sure, don't you, before you let a boy know you care about him?"

"Very, very sure, Penny."

"Well, I'm only eighteen—eighteen-and-a-half," she corrected with her same honesty. "Terry and I have fun. We fight, but we have fun. I'd be pretty sunk, I've discovered, if anyone else got him—but I have to take that chance. Being an actress is more important."

"Then I'd call that a pretty good answer to yourself, Pen. It doesn't look as if you are very deeply in love yet."

"It doesn't?" Penny's eyes glowed with relief. "I thought that's the way it is," she nodded, "but I knew you'd know for sure."

She gave him a grateful kiss and he knew that no time or space could ever separate him from Penny.

"Now listen," she said to Terry when she finally got down to the drawing room and was removing a rope of smilax he had wound about his neck like a boa constrictor, "you're interfering with the decorators."

"But the guy in the white pants told me to hook it above the mantel," he protested.

"Well, hook it." She held a ladder for him but turned as David rushed in.

"I can't find my bride," David shouted. "I've looked every place."

"You won't find her today." Penny left Terry to his fate on the ladder while she elaborated sparingly: "That's custom, Davy. You don't see each other until the wedding."

"No?"

"Sure." Penny hitched up her slacks, tucked in her shirt and returned to her ladder.

"She's right, David." Faith pushed him aside to set a bowl of roses on a table, and the decorator who was turning the marble mantel into an altar, confirmed it.

"There isn't much place for a groom on his wedding day," he remarked jocularly. "Why don't you go out and take a walk?"

"Nuts." David clumped to the kitchen where caterers were unpacking a large carton. "Here, I'll

GLORY BE!

give you a hand," he offered. But Trudy's voice warned:

"Be careful, Mr. David. The weddin' cake's on that table behind you. You's abackin' into it." And his mother's voice called from the butler's pantry:

"Go take off that good blouse, darling, before you ruin it."

David turned and looked at the wedding cake. Its four tiers rose in white fluting and flowers, and it was topped by a bell tied with tulle. He hungered for a thick slice and that reminded him of his sabre that Carrol would use to cut it.

He hurried out to the garage; saw his canvas kit sitting in the driveway beside a neat row of luggage that he supposed belonged to Carrol; and heard his father say:

"Back her out now, Parker. I'll load up while you go on with the polishing."

"Is my sabre in there?" he asked.

The car came out slowly with his father and Parker pushing, and Colonel Parrish extended a restraining hand when David stepped up to help. "Look out, the car has wax on it," he warned. "Gerald took your sabre upstairs."

"Thanks. Thanks very much." David said it stiffly and he walked just as stiffly back to the house. With no immediate destination in mind he thought he should make sure of the sabre, so he went upstairs. He could hear voices in Carrol's room and he set his lips forcefully, stalked to the closed door, and gave a weak knock. "Could I come in?" he begged.

Shrieks were his only answer until Denise eased through a crack to him. "David, you can't see Carrol today," she explained, as if he didn't know. "Not until the wedding."

"Well, could I talk to her? Through the door, I mean."

Denise slid back and a discussion followed.

"Of course, you can talk to me, Davy." Carrol's voice sounded very sweet on the other side of the wood. "I'd come out but they're all enjoying this foolishness so much I thought it doesn't matter. Is there anything you want?"

"Yes." David thought of adding "you" but as quickly dismissed it. "No, everything's okay," he said bravely; then he added like a small boy: "But I'm lonesome. There isn't anything for me to do."

"Well, find Penny. We need her up here, anyway. And pack the car, and see that the decorators are doing a good job. That should keep you busy until lunch time."

He saw no help in telling her that the drawing room was already a garden, that his father was masterfully in charge of the car; and as he still had left the finding of Penny, he went back downstairs.

She was in the sun room with Terry, sitting on

the tiled floor and eating ice cream and cake. A litter of boxes trailed smilax, and every chair held its arms protectively around great masses of flowers. "Come on in and have some boodle," Penny invited, peeking around a potted palm.

"Where'd you get the cake?" David eyed Penny's plate hungrily and she crawled to a coffee table and pushed a small bell.

"From the dream boxes. There are a hundred of them in the pantry and as there'll only be about forty guests, Terry and I helped ourselves. There's gobs of chicken salad if you want it."

"I'll take the works." David looked around for a place to sit, and at Terry's suggestion accepted the floor with a bamboo chair for a back-rest and white gladiolas for a background. He ate heartily and it was some time before he noticed that the conversation was in need of resuscitation. "I didn't interrupt anything, did I?" he asked belatedly.

"Nothing important." Terry set his plate down beside him and searched through his pockets for a cigarette. "I was just trying to interest Penny in taking a 'miniature,' " he said.

"No sale, huh?"

"Not a chance. She's still the career girl, although she did say that in five or ten years if she hasn't anything better to do . . ."

"Oh, Terry, keep still." Penny bounced her plate

against her knee and the spoon flew off. "David! Your blouse!" she cried. "Did it hit you?"

"Thank heavens, no." David gave her back the spoon, saying to Terry in the voice of one who knows: "Take my advice and rejoice that she turned you down. There isn't any girl worth what I'm going through today but Carrol—and I wouldn't do it again even for her."

Penny answered tartly: "You know you love it, David." She saw Denise in the door and waved her in.

"So here you are," Denise said. "We sent David for you ages ago."

"Sorry." David looked up ruefully over a bite of cake. "I'm in such a twitchet, you know, with so much on my mind . . ."

But Denise paid no attention to him. "We forgot 'the something old, something new, something borrowed, something blue,' " she said to Penny. "Have you got anything old that Carrol could wear?"

"Plenty." Penny began a singsong of "old rags, old clothes, old shoes" then broke off to cry: "Mums has the very thing: a handkerchief her grandmother made. Sit down and have some food."

"Wait until I tell Faith, so she'll stop pawing through our closets. Order a plate for her, too."

The circle in the sun room grew, and inspired by the grand piano that rolled into their midst, Penny beat out a one-fingered wedding march.

"Tum, tum, te tum," they sang with her, spurred on by David's unhappy face, until Terry pushed her from the bench and a chorus of song followed his crashing chords.

"Couldn't I please come in?" a plaintive voice called from the hall.

"You most certainly cannot!" Penny jumped up, saw David in the act of rising too, and gave him a backward push before she bounded out the door. She took Carrol firmly by the arm and propelled her up the stairs.

"But you're all having such fun. I want to be in it, too."

"I know it doesn't seem quite fair, but it was an accident," Penny comforted. "We'll send David out of the house and then you can roam around as much as you like. Have you had lunch?"

"Not yet. Elfreda said she'd bring it but that's the last I saw of her."

"We kept her too busy. Go on up; I'll bring it." Penny ran back to the kitchen, and still feeling hungry herself, ordered two trays.

When she returned, allowing herself an even smaller crack in the door than Denise had managed, she announced that Perkins was on his way; then stopped with clasped hands. "Oh, darling, the dress is divine!" she breathed; going over to the filmy net bridal gown that was being modeled by a headless dressmaker's form. Its train was spread into a fan on a sheet; its accompanying veil hung from a milliner's standard. "The veil is even more beautiful than I thought it could be when I saw it being made." Penny touched the coronet of tiny curled ostrich feathers and orange blossoms, and lifted the short face veil. "How does this thing work?" she asked. "I want to be sure it will come off when I pull it."

Carrol came over to demonstrate the veil. "There's an orange blossom on the end of a thread," she showed Penny. "You pull it gently and the whole front piece drops off."

"I hope I don't pull off the works." Penny was dubious as she gave a practice twitch.

"Is David all right?"

"Yes, Mike and Dick finally showed up and Terry got tired of interior decorating, and what do you suppose they're doing? Swimming. David's swimming on his wedding day. Did you ever hear of anything so silly?"

Carrol went to the window and looked out. She could hear voices by the pool and she leaned forward to peer through the trees but Penny pulled her back. "Play fair," she cautioned. "You can't look at David, either."

"All right." Carrol agreed, but she wondered miserably if it would ever, ever be four o'clock.

By mid-afternoon the bridesmaids were in a flutter.

They could hear cars stopping before the door, and voices drifted up to them, mingled with the soft strains of an orchestra.

"I lose everything I touch," Faith sighed. "I had a shoe horn on the dresser—oh, Penny took it." She hopped down the hall on one foot and stopped at Carrol's door to look in.

Mrs. Parrish was there, exquisitely lovely in cream lace, and Penny, still clad in a housecoat, was down on the floor unfolding yards and yards of bridal veil. Carrol stood in the center of the sheet, her arms raised for Elfreda to adjust the cascading folds of net and her head bent to receive the coronet Mrs. Parrish was holding above her curls.

"Ask Denise to come for a minute, too," Carrol said as Faith limped around her, viewing her from all sides. "And Penny, please hand me the packages from the table."

"I can't tell you all how much I love you," she said when the girls were grouped around her. "But think of me when you wear these." She passed out the tissue-papered boxes and watched while they tore off the wrappings. Friendship pins lay on cotton, and the twisted knot that linked two golden hearts was made of diamonds.

"Oh, thank you, lamb!" Penny cried. "Of course, I knew all about it, having helped you select them—but I adore mine."

"They're beautiful, Carrol." Faith and Denise caressed their gifts and she bent forward to kiss them.

"Be careful not to get lipstick on her cheek," Mrs. Parrish warned from the floor where she had bent to finish Penny's task. "Now, run and dress. You too, Penny, or you'll never be ready."

She stood up, looking at Carrol gravely. "My very lovely daughter," she said with a catch in her voice. "Nothing can ever make me happier than I am to-day."

"Thank you, Aunt Marjorie." Carrol had no thought for her dress or the veil when she reached out her arms. "You don't know what it means to have a really, truly mother."

When Mrs. Parrish had gone downstairs to see to their guests and Penny was running busily between the bathroom and the dressing table, Carrol stepped from her sheet and said: "Penny, will you do something for me?"

"Of course, darling." Penny looked from the mirror and smiled. "What?"

"I want to go to Daddy's room now; to his little sitting room. Will you ask one of the maids to come for me there, when it's—it's time?"

"Why, yes, but . . ." She watched Carrol gathering up her veil and said anxiously: "But won't it hurt too much?"

"No." Carrol shook her head. "Daddy's wedding

gift is there. His lawyer brought it to me and I wanted to open it there. I'll be ready in time." She kissed Penny swiftly, said: "Don't worry, Pen," then gathered the mass of net and tulle into her arms.

The door to Langdon Houghton's room stood open, as it always had. Carrol slipped in and let the latch click shut behind her. "Daddy?" she whispered, "Oh, Daddy darling, I need you so today." Only the silence answered her and she went slowly toward the desk, where just a few short months ago his smile had always welcomed her. "I'm going away with David," she said, running her fingers over the smooth carved back of his chair. "I'm leaving our house for a little while. But I'm not leaving you, Daddy." Through her tears she saw his books; his pencils in the tray she had made for him at camp; his tobacco jar. She touched them all lovingly then knelt before a drawer in the desk and took out a large manila envelope. It held a purple velvet case, worn, its clasp old-fashioned, and a letter. The strong handwriting caught at her heart but she rested her hands on the arm of the chair and slowly unfolded the page.

My darling little daughter,

This is our very happy day. My gift to you is your mother's string of pearls; her wedding pearls. Wear them, honey, and be happy. Be always as beautiful and lovely as you are today.

Daddy.

She opened the case slowly. The strand of pearls, mellowed and creamy from the touch of her mother's young throat, lay on the faded velvet. She slipped the note into the empty place they had left and held the pearls to her lips. She could hear the faint strains of her wedding march and as she fastened the clasp about her neck, there was a timid knock on the door.

When she turned the knob, music swelled into the room. She dropped her train, and too softly for the kneeling maid to hear, whispered: "I'm ready, Daddy."

Downstairs a hush had fallen on the guests who waited in the drawing room. The fireplace had been massed in green. Tall white tapers glowed in the foliage above sprays of Easter lilies, and palms were banked in a wide arc behind two white satin pillows. Mrs. Parrish saw her husband follow the chaplain to the altar and she slipped through silent groups to stand beside him. The soft strains of Lohengrin's beautiful wedding march filled the air, and as he touched her arm she was conscious that Tippy was pressed against her, too. She saw David come from the library walking soberly beside Michael. He smiled briefly at her before he turned toward the stairway, the world forgotten, as he watched for Carrol.

Dear David, she thought, loving him so much. Then she too, turned to look at Faith who was walking slowly across the hall. Faith was lovely in her shell-pink gown. The foamy net trailed behind her and from under a pale pink hat she looked down at the roses she carried. It *had* to be a pink wedding, Marjorie Parrish thought, because Carrol loves pink as much as Penny does. . . . She felt the sting of tears but only took a deep breath and lifted her head higher. Faith had reached the altar; Denise was halfway there, and Penny stood in the doorway . . . Penny, in soft rose. Her brown curls cascaded to her shoulders beneath a filmy rosy halo and her brown eyes held a smile. The toe of each sandal tipped rhythmically from under her long skirt until she reached the altar where she turned with the others. Mrs. Parrish saw her eyes meet Terry's; saw the long look that passed between them and her throat tightened. The tears welled up and she bent her head.

"Miz Parrish, honey." Trudy's work-worn hand reached out, held hers with loving strength, and she felt herself drawn against Trudy's stiff white apron. It covered the new blue dress and Trudy was saying softly: "Look up, honey. Miss Carrol's comin' down the stairs."

"I can't, Trudy."

"She's on the landin' now," Trudy's voice went on. "The sunlight's shinin' behind her till you almost think it's an angel standin' there. An' Mr. David's lookin' at her with his heart in his eyes."

Mrs. Parrish gave a stifled sob and Trudy's voice was tender. "Don't cry," she said gently. "I know you's thinkin' that little Miss Carrol ought to have her father with her. But it's all right. Mr. David jes' can't wait—he's gone to meet her."

"He has? Oh, bless him, Trudy." She tried to stop the tears that came too fast.

"Look up, Miz Parrish," Trudy begged. "They's comin' on together. An' the sun's shinin' on 'em, an' . . . Oh, honey, it would make your heart so glad to see 'em . . . cause they's awalkin' in glory."